Sanctum, Book 1

Brenna
Lyons

Dream Walk

This book is written in US English.

PUBLISHER

Chapter One

"Have you recovered well from your nightmare, Rachel?" Jaden expected Rachel to concede defeat, however grudgingly. She was his mate, and his ability to walk her dreams without an invitation to do so proved it.

The look of venom she shot him announced the fight wasn't over yet. Her words sank in slowly.

"I didn't have a nightmare, Jaden. Lying about this won't work. Call in a Truth-Sayer, if you wish. Or a Mind Healer. Either one can testify to the fact I am being truthful. You are not my mate."

Jaden opened his mouth to protest the accusation that he was being underhanded, and she offered her palm in silent order to keep quiet.

"I don't care what the Mage Prophet said, and I don't care that you and my father believe her. She. Is. Wrong." With that, Rachel rose smoothly and sauntered out of the room.

Jaden wanted to shake the truth from her. He wanted to growl and shout, to throw the crystal tableware against the wall, and maybe even to hit someone. Hard.

Reeve sighed. "You walked her dreams without an invitation to do so?"

"Yes, I did."

Reeve shot a scowl after his daughter. "There really isn't a question then."

He offered Rachel's father a weak smile. "Thank you for believing me." If Reeve thought he'd lied, life would get complicated quickly. As Mage Lord, Reeve had the power to banish Jaden from Sanctum without even waiting for a trying by the Truth-Sayer.

"The Mage Prophet is never wrong, Jaden. Rachel is your mate. Sooner or later, she must accept that."

A new idea occurred to him. "They're not wrong, but they don't always tell us the whole story. They offer puzzles and riddles as well as facts."

Reeve leaned toward him. "What are you thinking?"

"What if..." He was being presumptuous, he was sure.

"Go on?" Reeve steepled his fingers and sat back in his chair.

Jaden took a drink of his coffee, composing himself. "What if Rachel hasn't been ready to be my mate until now? What if my dream walk is the first indication that she might be *becoming* ready?"

Reeve's brow furrowed. "In what way?"

"Perhaps her powers are evolving...changing somehow. Some young mages develop additional powers or expand them in their mid to late twenties." *That might be why neither of Reeve's children—nor either of his granddaughters—have displayed the Lord's power yet.*

"The Mage Healers said Rachel's powers had set. There is no fluctuation." There was a note of finality in that, a warning that Reeve would not stand for further discussion on the matter.

"Not her powers then," Jaden conceded. "A precipitating event, perhaps?"

Reeve tensed minutely. "Of what sort?"

"I don't know," he admitted.

There was a moment of tense silence. "I will seek answers from the Mage Prophet this Worship Day."

Jaden tipped his head in thanks and took his leave. There was no possibility Rachel would choose to spend more time with him today.

****

"Come back here, you little bitch!"

Lara ran faster, her body aching, her lungs and heart working hard. Day and night, awake and asleep, she ran from him. How did Gart keep finding her?

On one level, Lara knew she was dreaming. She should be able to snap herself out of this or rewrite the dream, since it was lucid dreaming. Somehow, she had done so the night before, but she didn't know how.

If I did, I would repeat it. Anything has to be better than running from Gart in my dreams, even lack of sleep.

On another level, Lara knew dreams weren't safe. Gart could track her in dreams. He *was* tracking her in dreams.

And I have awakened with injuries he inflicts before.

"You're mine, Lara. You know you're mine."

Oh, Mother. How could you do this to me?

In twenty-six years, her mother hadn't mentioned a word about the betrothal. At the reading of her mother's will, the magar had revealed the document her mother had signed on the day of Lara's birth.

According to the magar, it was unbreakable. Lara was promised in marriage to a man nearly twice her age. She'd guess he was; in truth, Lara was basing that on Gart's appearance. She knew nothing about him but his cruelty and his name, so all she could do was guess.

That and his legal claim on me. In essence, Gart *owned* Lara. She and everything that was hers—meager as that was—was his.

But not the opposite.

"I will find you. I will not be denied," he warned.

Gart appeared before her as if by magic, his hand closing around her wrist and tightening.

Lara wrenched against his hold, desperate to escape him. She didn't question what Gart was doing. They'd played this game for almost two weeks.

As if in confirmation, he chuckled darkly. "New York. You thought you could lose yourself in a crowd?"

Her breathing went strangled, and Lara shook her head. He'd tracked her again. She had to move.

Fast. Lara didn't question where she'd go. She'd simply run. *As far as the money will go, and then I'll walk.* Anything that kept Gart away from her was what she would have to do.

As if he could pick that thought from her mind, Gart's face hardened. "Stay where you are, Lara. Don't make this more difficult than it has to be."

That unglued her tongue. "Difficult? I have crossed half the world to escape a madman intent on—"

He slapped her hard enough to send flashes of color through her field of vision. The copper tang of blood invaded her mouth.

Gart opened his mouth to say something, but a roar of rage eclipsed it. His hand loosened, and he turned away.

Lara didn't waste time wondering what was happening. She was momentarily free. Her heart pounding in fear, she ran.

When I wake, I'll have to run in the physical world. He'd touched her. He knew where she was.

****

His enemy recoiled, ducking Jaden's blow.

A mocking smile curved the man's lips. "A little Dream-Walker," he taunted. "Did she call for help, Dream-Walker?"

"Clearly," he lied. *His energy is mage in nature. He's not a part of Rachel's dream; he's an invader in it. He knows I'm a Dream-Walker. As long as he doesn't know I'm Rachel's mate, I have an advantage.*

Jaden's mind worked at this complication. He'd thought Rachel's nightmare had been a natural dream. It wasn't, which left him with the questions of who the mage was and how he found his way into Rachel's dreams. For that matter, what sort of rogue terrorized another this way?

Rogue! That was the answer. Whoever he was and whatever his aim, he was no doubt a rogue out for revenge against Reeve, using Rachel to find it.

"You have no business here, Dream-Walker." There was a threat couched in that.

"She asked for my aid. That *is* my business, by design of the Goddess Mother Herself."

"How old are you, boy?" He sneered at Jaden. "Thirty...at most?"

"It is of no consequence, rogue." It was, if the mage he faced was markedly older. *If his powers have matured into a master mage's abilities.*

5

As if in answer, his opponent materialized a scythe. It wasn't a young mage's power. A mage would have to be twice Jaden's twenty-nine years to do that.

At least.

A scythe. A scythe is a Tracker's weapon. So, he's a Tracker.

"Stay and die, Dream-Walker."

The weapon arced toward Jaden, and he dodged too slowly. The slice across his bicep was excruciating, nearly painful enough to make Jaden lose his concentration.

That was unacceptable. If he lost concentration, Jaden would be catapulted out of Rachel's dream realm, and that would leave her defenseless against the rogue.

The next two arcs missed entirely, but Jaden admitted to himself that he was outmatched. This was an old and accomplished mage who wasn't adverse to the idea of killing him.

Jaden needed help. He needed—

Rachel!

He didn't translocate to her within the dream realm, as he should have. Jaden sidestepped another blow, confused by his failure. This was Rachel's dream. If she'd awakened, he would have been catapulted to his own dream world. A Tracker didn't have the power to bind Jaden in the dream realm or to siphon his powers, no matter how accomplished he was.

Then why did I fail?

At a loss to explain it, Jaden pictured Rachel as he'd seen her moments ago. He reached his consciousness out into the construct of her dream, snagged her essence...

And translocated.

She hit him at a run, and they went down together in a tangle of limbs. A panicked little shout left her lips, and she raised her head to stare at him, her blue eyes going wide. Her face paled around the rising bruise the rogue had left.

"W-who are you?" she asked. "I know you. The beach...last night—"

A roar let Jaden know the Tracker was in motion and closing on them.

"Who is he, Rachel? Who is the Tracker?" *And why haven't you told your father about this?*

She tried to push away from him, and Jaden held her close. They had no time for games. Didn't she know that?

"Answer me, Rachel," he demanded. "Who is he?" There was no question Jaden would need Reeve's help, and knowing their shared enemy was essential.

"Let me go. He's coming. Can't you feel it?" Her eyes went wide and wild, and her struggling increased.

The Tracker barreled toward them from the dark recesses of her dreaming mind, and Jaden translocated them away. He cursed his inability to change her dream parameters with the Tracker fully engaged on his prey. If Jaden was older, he would be unparalleled in this realm. He would be able to evict the Tracker from her dream and even to wake Rachel from dreamtime to protect her.

"Who is he, Rachel? I must know, so I can stop him."

She glared at him, an expression he knew well. "I'm. Not. Rachel."

"What?" If she didn't think she was Rachel, who did she think she was? And why would she not recognize herself in her own dream realm? Was it some trick?

If it was, how would the Tracker trick her dream self into the delusion? Short of him working with a rogue Illusionist, there was no way Jaden knew of to manage that.

She started struggling more earnestly. "Let me go!"

The Tracker reappeared, grumbling curses. Jaden translocated them again.

"He's engaged now. He'll find us faster every time I translocate us," he warned her.

"Exactly. Let me go." Rachel tried to push him off.

Jaden hoisted her up with him, wincing at the kick to his shin. "Stop that," he growled. "Rachel, use your powers. When he shows up again, siphon his powers. Leave him helpless, and I can stop him." *At least for tonight.*

"I can't do that," she snapped. "And, I'm *not* Rachel."

The Tracker headed for them with a battle cry that warned he was going to kill Jaden at his first opportunity.

"What can you do?" Jaden countered, bracing himself for another jump. Surely, her delusion didn't include her being powerless, trapped in a dream without her magic. Whatever she believed she could do was as real in here as her actual magic was in the physical world.

Rachel gaped at him for a moment. Her gaze snapped to the Tracker, and she wrenched her left hand from Jaden's grasp. Before he could translocate them again, the outlay of her magic stunned him to stillness.

The Tracker flew the opposite direction with a grunt of pain. In the distance, something that sounded like glass crashed. The dream melted to a mist that told Jaden she was semiconscious. His hands were abruptly empty, as she took the first steps toward consciousness.

Realization was a moment behind. She'd woken herself by breaking something in the physical world with her magic.

The Lord's power. Either Rachel was developing new powers, or this really wasn't Rachel.

Perhaps not. He couldn't state it definitively until he was certain. Perhaps Rachel had locked onto her father's power in her befuddled state. It was a dream, after all, and she could use whatever she believed was real within the dream.

I have to get her out of here before the Tracker returns. The answers to all his questions could wait.

"Wake now," he ordered her. "But call for me when you fear the Tracker is near. My name is Jaden."

She whispered it back to him.

And woke.

Jaden levered his eyes open, trembling, bathed in sweat. He pushed from the bed, his arm complaining the still-weeping wound the Tracker had inflicted in her dream.

He was weak from the outlay of magic and in need of rest, but visions of Rachel covered in bruises haunted him. If the Tracker had marked her as well—which he didn't doubt—he would have his proof.

And reason enough to kill the rogue.

Jaden scooped his boots from the floor and headed into the rising sun.

Chapter Two

Jaden pounded on Reeve's door, unsure which to hope for. If Rachel had the bruises, her life was in danger, and she had no memory of it to help them find the Tracker. If she didn't, his mate was unprotected in the world, and he had no clue who and where she was.

He added another fact to the grim list. If it wasn't Rachel, Reeve was under no obligation to help Jaden stop the Tracker, and he couldn't do it alone.

Frustrated by that fact, he pounded on the door again. Halfway through his staccato drumming, the door swung wide, and Reeve glared at him.

His gaze traveled up and down Jaden's body, and his eyes narrowed. "Jaden? What is it?"

"I need to see Rachel. Now. It's urgent."

Reeve waved him in. "If you've come in your bedclothes, stinking of sweat and magic, bleeding... It must be."

"Really, Jaden," Rachel complained from the darkened stairwell. "Isn't it bad enough that I am subjected to your company at all daylight hours? Now you pound the door down when the sun hasn't cleared the hills."

His heart pounding, Jaden cleared his throat. "Would you turn up the lights, my Lord?"

Reeve hurried to do so. He flicked his wrist and made an upward motion of his hand. When the lamps were burning brightly, Jaden examined Rachel's appearance. Her cheek and wrist were unblemished.

Her blue eyes widened in seeming shock. "What is it? What has happened to you?" There was something cautious in that...something guarded.

A lump burning in his throat, Jaden strode to Rachel. He reached up and unclasped the promise necklace she'd worn since Rachel was a toddler and the Mage Prophet had foretold their union.

He bowed reverently. "I apologize for the confusion, Rachel...and for disturbing your sleep. I had to be certain. You are not my mate."

She didn't answer. Jaden offered another bow and turned away.

"Thank you." Her voice was soft, a voice a man could easily fall in love with, the voice he'd prayed for years he'd hear directed at him.

But she was the wrong woman for Jaden. The wrong voice for him to harking to, no matter how alike the two women looked and sounded. He headed for the door, intent on finding the correct one.

Reeve blocked his way. "Are you certain?" he asked.

"Wherever my mate is, she's injured and in danger." He glanced back at Rachel. "Your daughter was correct, my Lord. She's not my mate."

More information took its place in his rioting mind. "They are alike in looks and voice, but they are not the same woman. I am sure of it."

"But the Mage Prophet said—"

"I intend to learn why she said it," Jaden assured him. "A Mage Prophet wouldn't be fooled by the similarities. It is her magic not to be misled by such insignificant details." He started moving. Perhaps Jaden would pound down another door this morning.

11

Reeve grasped his arm, restraining Jaden gently. "We will go together. A Mage Healer and fresh clothing. Then we will both learn why we were misled this way."

He took a moment to calm himself, then nodded his agreement. For the moment, Reeve had an investment in helping him. Jaden wouldn't do anything to risk that.

****

The Mage Prophet was an ancient mage, more than a century old. Clothed in bright-colored robes, her wrinkled face and hands looked like old parchment.

The air was thick and heavy with incense and wood smoke, though the sun had barely risen. It was an unseemly hour to visit, but the Mage Prophet appeared unperturbed by it.

"You expected us, Prophet," Jaden guessed.

"Call me Abbigell." Her voice was sweet and rich, nearly hypnotic. "Sit, please."

She motioned toward the many chairs and lounges in the large room. No doubt, the choice one made gave insights the Mage Prophet could use. Neither Jaden nor Reeve made a move toward them.

No doubt, that tells her something, as well.

She smiled and lifted a glass of dark liquid to her lips, sipping slowly. There was seemingly no urgency to learn why they were here.

Jaden opened his mouth to address the issue.

Reeve beat him to the finish line. "You gave a false prophecy," the Mage Lord informed her coolly.

Abbigell placed the glass on the tabletop without a hint of sound. Her smile never faltered. "You only believe I have."

Reeve took a decisive step toward her. "You told me Jaden's mate was Rachel."

"I said no such thing." She waved her hand in a dismissive gesture then motioned for silence before Reeve could explode. "I said, my Lord, that Jaden would take your eldest female heir as mate."

Reeve's face went crimson, and his mouth worked at words that fought emerging. When they broke free, they were akin to a roar. "Rachel *is* my eldest female heir."

"Is she now?" she taunted.

Jaden waved Reeve off, latching on the game at last. "*Isn't* she?"

"You know the answer to that already, Dream-Walker, do you not?" Abbigell raised the index finger of her left hand and pressed the tip of the right index finger to it. "Fact number one... Mage Prophets never give false prophecies." The middle finger joined the index finger, and she moved her pointing digit to that one. "Fact number two... Your mate is the Mage Lord's eldest female heir." The ring finger. "Since you have reasoned—quite correctly, may I add—that his eldest female heir is not young Rachel, it must be someone else."

Reeve's anger uncorked. "You go too far, Prophet."

She smiled serenely.

"I should know where I have planted my seed," he thundered.

"I am certain you do," she conceded.

"Only Daza has borne for me."

Abbigell sipped her tea, seemingly unconcerned that she'd angered the Mage Lord so acutely.

"Daza has not borne for another."

"Certainly not," she replied, as if the very suggestion of it offended her as much as it offended Reeve. Abbigell didn't point out that a child Daza bore for another would not be Reeve's heir and would be immaterial. That went without saying.

"But not a proclamation of 'certainly not' for me?"

"A male's involvement is easily hidden," she noted, as if she wasn't accusing Reeve of having an illegitimate child.

"There is no way to hide a child born in the sanctum," he continued.

She tipped her head in agreement.

"Mated or not, everyone knows the parentage of a mage child."

She chuckled. "Born *inside* Sanctum, you mean," she corrected gently.

Reeve's hands tightened into fists, as if he was considering doing Abbigell physical harm. His words came through clenched teeth. "I have never sacked in with a human woman. No mage sacks—" He stopped cold at Abbigell's wide smile.

Reeve turned his head and stared at Jaden. It didn't take more than a few heartbeats for Jaden to decipher Reeve's line of thinking.

Jaden sighed. "No *responsible* mage would sack in with a human."

Reeve grumbled what was probably a curse. "Darren."

****

Reeve's son had never been mistaken for a responsible adult. At fifty-six, Darren hadn't chosen to settle down with his mate. Jaden wasn't entirely certain Darren had even chosen to seek out a mate.

Darren had sired two illegitimate children in the sanctum. The idea that they weren't the first wouldn't come as a shock to anyone in Sanctum. Only the fact that this one was half-human would be noteworthy.

In retrospect, it was amazing that it had taken them so long to focus on Darren as a suspect in siring an heir they hadn't known about.

In a rare show of self-preservation, Darren answered the door promptly at Reeve's knock. Of course, he was dressed in nothing but a loose pair of sleeping pants that showed he was erect.

Reeve shouldered past his son without a greeting but grumbling something that sounded suspiciously like "Keep it in your pants, for once."

If the situation hadn't been so serious, Jaden would have laughed at that. Instead, he followed Reeve into the house and stretched out on the closest lounge.

It was an insufferably rude move, but—considering Darren's antics had not only put Jaden's mate at risk but also had caused Jaden to lose sleep and blood—Jaden was less than concerned that he might be considered rude.

Darren stood an arm's length away from him, his brow furrowed, probably working at Jaden's atypical lack of manners.

"Tell us about the human woman," Jaden ordered, his head aching. He rubbed the grit from his eyes and focused on Darren.

Reeve's son slid into a deep, soft chair without even a hint of embarrassment, fear, or any other appropriate emotion. "*Which* human woman?" he taunted.

Reeve glared at him. "How many, Darren?"

"Over the years?" He paused long enough to make Jaden tense. "A dozen. Fifteen, maybe?"

Jaden felt his stomach drop out in shock and disbelief.

"Maybe?" Reeve shouted. "Dear Goddess, you don't even know where you plant your seed?" That part was certainly news to Reeve. Though Darren had illegitimate children, it hadn't been apparent that he was indiscriminate before.

Jaden cut the Mage Lord off before he could continue into a lecture that would get them no closer to the information they needed. "This one would have been more than twenty-four years ago. That should narrow it down a bit."

It offered only a decade for Darren to have been actively seeking beds, instead of the full three and a half decades he'd been doing so.

"It does," Darren agreed.

Thank the Goddess!

"To whom?" Reeve inquired coolly.

Darren's look of confusion was nearly comical. "Their *names*?"

"How many?" Jaden countered before Reeve could explode again.

Darren shifted, looking discomfited for the first time. "Nine? Ten? Maybe?"

That was Reeve's breaking point. "Ten? You broke with the mores and sacked in with human women ten times in as many years?"

"Well...more than ten times, but some of them warranted more than a single night of investigation."

Reeve's expression made it clear he had a lot more to say on the subject.

Jaden cut him off again. "So we have ten possible mothers for your eldest daughter."

Darren sighed. "The early days were pretty crazy, as the humans would say. I was young and imp—" His head snapped around, his face losing color. "My what? You mean *elder* daughter, and Juniatta is her mother, as you well know."

"Do I?" he challenged.

Darren went an alarming shade of gray. He shot a panicked look at his father.

"And you don't know any of their names," Jaden continued, driving the situation home.

He swallowed hard. "I remember *one* name." If he was a child, Jaden would have called his tone puerile.

Reeve's brows rose. "Well, wasn't she special?"

Darren's expression went wistful. "She was, actually. Alanna was...more than any man deserves in a woman. I was starting to believe she was my mate."

"And then?" Reeve prompted him, his voice gentler than it had been moments before.

His eyes closed, and Darren laid his head back on the chair, looking prematurely aged at the memory. "She disappeared between two of my visits...without a trace."

Reeve and Jaden stared at each other. Jaden didn't doubt they were thinking the same thing. A renegade Tracker was stalking Darren's daughter, and one of her probable mothers had disappeared. Alanna was likely the mother they sought, and the Tracker might have been responsible for her disappearance.

"I suggest we start there," Jaden opined. "We should find out everything we can about Alanna."

"Better than nothing," Reeve agreed.

Darren didn't move. "How do you know I have a daughter in the human realm?"

Jaden didn't hesitate. "She's my mate."

He winced, but Darren didn't voice whatever his concern was. If it was the fact that Jaden had broken with mores to tell Darren what they were to each other at this inappropriate moment, he could be damned. For most of Jaden's life, people had harbored the expectation that he was fated to Rachel. That was no less inappropriate.

"She's in danger. And, like it or not, you're going to help me find her, Darren." Jaden let the threat hang between them.

Reeve wasn't content to let it end there. "Clear your social calendar," he commanded.

Darren didn't raise his head, though his eyes opened. "I will help in any way I can. You have my vow on that."

Jaden eased back fully on the lounge, half-listening as Reeve started interrogating his son about his favorite lover. Their voices buzzed in the background of Jaden's mind.

{Jaden?}

He startled awake at the sound of his mate's mental voice, then cursed the reaction.

"What is it?" Darren was abruptly at his side.

Jaden waved him off, then concentrated on sending himself into a trance state. Once there, he reached for her essence...

And jumped to her side.

She was there. Jaden searched their surroundings, searching for clues of where she was.

A bus. Most likely where she is in the physical world, at the moment. *Sleeping on a bus.*

"Can I trust Jaden?" she mused.

Chapter Three

Lara fought to keep her eyes open, but the passing of nondescript scenery and hum of the bus engine were lulling her to sleep.

Not to mention how exhausted I am. Calculating how long it had been since she'd had a full night of sleep was an exercise in futility. With her brain operating on two pistons out of six, Lara wasn't certain what day it was, let alone what day she'd slept decently.

It could be worse. At least she was moving. If she hadn't slipped out of the dingy little motel room unnoticed, they would have jailed her for the destruction her telekinesis had caused. Trapped in a cell, only blocks from where Gart expected to find her, would make it far too easy for him.

Sleep will make it easy.

But her vision was jumping and blurring in exhaustion. Lara rubbed her eyes, pleading for a little more time before sleep won out.

She didn't fully understand why Gart could track her more effectively while she slept. Whatever the reason, Lara was thankful she was hidden or masked or fogged during her waking hours.

I could call the other one. Jaden...

Visions of him danced behind her still-closed eyelids. Jaden was about her own age, she'd guess. His hair was black as a moonless night and his blue eyes only a few shades lighter than that.

Even when he'd refused to release her, Jaden hadn't hurt her. He hadn't asked for or demanded anything from her.

Why? If he didn't want something, why had he helped her?

He said he wanted to protect me. But why would he want to?

There was a more pressing problem. *Can I trust Jaden?*

"Yes. You can."

His voice unnerved her, and Lara turned toward him in the seat. They were still on the bus, but the backpack she'd set on the window seat was nowhere to be seen, while Jaden had taken its place.

She swiveled her head, looking around the bus. The seats opposite their positions were empty. There had been a mother and her toddler son there moments earlier. A peek up the aisle showed the driver's seat was unoccupied, and the steering wheel was turning on its own, following the road flawlessly.

I've fallen asleep again. When had she? How long had Gart been tracking her?

"Don't think his name," Jaden cautioned. "It will help him track you."

"How do I know you're not a figment of my imagination?" *Or a trick Gart has started using to make me think I don't have to run?*

The sudden darkness had her searching the skies. Rain clouds had been nowhere in sight moments before, but they now blocked the sun. In the distance, lightning crashed. Thunder rumbled a warning, and Lara shivered.

"I told you not to think his name. Don't say it or picture his face either. All of that helps him hone in on you." Jaden shifted, moving his gaze from the sky to her. "Ask me to protect you, and I can shield you from him."

"How do I know you're not a figment of my imagination?" she repeated.

A smile curved his full lips and lit his eyes, leaving her squirming...but not in fear. His voice was dark and rich.

"I could prove I'm as real as the Tracker is, but I don't think you'll allow it."

"H-how?" Jaden didn't intend to hit her, did he?

He scowled. "Never."

Lightning flashed, highlighting his face. It was harsh but appealing.

I'm going insane.

"No," he breathed. "You're not going insane. Not at all."

"And you're reading my mind." It wasn't fair that he could do that when she had not a clue what was in his.

"We are *in* your mind. I am little more than a phantom here, but you are very real, as are your thoughts."

Lara nodded.

The next bolt of lightning was so close it made her eyes ache.

Jaden grasped her arm...and she blinked her eyes in the bright sunlight. The hand he wasn't holding plunged into warm sand, and Lara looked around at the beach in confusion.

She vaguely noted that it was the beach she'd seen in her dream two nights earlier. *When I first saw Jaden. Did he bring me back here for a reason?*

His hand inched away from her arm. "My apologies. The Tracker was getting too close. Once he sees or touches you, I cannot change the dream parameters.

"And no, I had no reason to bring you here but that it was convenient and already in the recesses of your mind to be utilized."

Lara glared at him. She wasn't sure how much more of him reading her mind and answering unspoken thoughts she could take.

Or dragging me from place to place this way.

Jaden sighed. "Ask for my help, and I can shield him out. If I do that, I will have no need to...drag you from place to place."

"But you can't shield him out unless I ask you?"

"No. I cannot force you to accept that." He paused a moment. "I wouldn't force you, even if I could."

The magar's face was grim. "It is unbreakable." He leaned toward her. "Do you intend to accept that?"

"That's the key, isn't it?" Lara asked urgently. "The magar knew refusing to accept the claim did...something. Not breaking it precisely, but something."

A cold wind blew in from the sea. Lara shivered.

"Accepting him gives him greater ability to track you and makes whatever the agreement is unbreakable."

"What does accepting you do?" she countered. There had to be a trick here somewhere. No one helped anyone else for nothing. Well, few did, anyway.

The sky went from blue to gray, and the wind whipped at their clothing.

"It protects you." There was just the slightest edge of anger in that.

Jaden grasped her hand, and a sun-dappled meadow appeared around them. Birds chirped merrily, and the sound of running water whispered from somewhere within the trees. This place was new to her, she was fairly certain.

"An old memory, I believe," Jaden supplied.

"And?" she asked.

"What are you asking?" He seemed genuinely perplexed.

For once. "What do you get out of helping me?"

"Nothing. I want to protect you."

It made no sense. "Are you bound by your word, as well?"

"Yes. I am. I vow that I will not lie to you. There. I am bound by my word. I vow to you that accepting my protection gives me no power over you."

Can I trust him? He said her word was binding. What if his wasn't?

"I cannot force you to trust me. You must make that choice for yourself."

"And...and trusting you means accepting your protection?"

His voice gentled, and his expression softened. "Yes."

"Nothing else?"

"Your name would help." There was a hint of humor in his tone.

The answer stuck in her throat. The old stories said there was power in a name. Her mother said there was always a kernel of truth in myths and wives' tales. Was that one of the truths?

Jaden sighed, seemingly weary. "Only for a Spellmaster. A simple name holds no power for either a Dream-Walker or a Tracker."

"You said we're in my mind. If that's true, why can't you pick my name from my thoughts?"

"People rarely think of themselves in the third person."

That made a certain amount of sense to her. *Gods help me. He's making sense. I must be more tired than I thought.*

Lara shook her head, trying to dislodge that thought. "How can you prove you're not a figment of my imagination?"

"Do you give me permission to?"

His expression went so potent, her heart stuttered. Heat seeped into her body, and pleasant shivers worked up and down her spine.

"Do you?" Jaden prompted.

"Yes." It came out little more than a gasp.

Jaden shifted toward her and lowered his face to the vee of her shirt. His lips were slightly parted, and his breath bathed the upper curve of her breasts.

It was so intimate, Lara found herself repeating—over and over—that it was just a dream.

"Not just," he replied.

In the next instant, Jaden was sucking gently at her skin. Lara let her head drop back, stunned by the acute pleasure he was giving her.

Her heart raced, and her head spun. She closed her fingers on the grass, seeking elusive balance.

His sucking became more insistent, the thundering of her pulse more urgent and primal. Lara brought one hand up and closed it in his hair.

What am I doing? It was insane to let Jaden do this.

He nipped at her, and Lara's supporting arm folded, depositing her on her elbow, breaking the connection between them. Jaden looked down at her, an unspoken challenge in his eyes.

Lara bit her lower lip lightly. It was a challenge she didn't know how to answer.

"However you want to," he replied, as if it was that simple.

Her mind rioted. If she knew what she wanted, Lara wasn't certain she was brave enough to ask for it.

"Tell me your name," Jaden requested.

Lara opened her mouth, closed it, then tried it again. Only the 'L' sound emerged before her voice failed her.

His jaw tightened, and he nodded in what appeared to be resignation. "Convince yourself that I'm real." Jaden reached down and started working the top few buttons on her shirt shut. "When we meet again, you'll have to decide whether or not you trust me." He met her gaze solidly. "The sooner, the better."

"Y-you're leaving me?" Why did the thought terrify her?

"When you wake, I return to myself."

"How are you going to wake me?"

"You are going to wake yourself."

Lara shook her head. "I can't. I've tried." The Freddy Kruger films were dead wrong; she couldn't even burn herself to shock herself awake.

"You did last night," he pointed out.

Her heart stuttered. "You mean...with my telekinesis." How many years had Lara hidden it? There must have been a reason her mother told her to hide it.

"It's not telekinesis, but that's not important right now. You're going to tell me what this unbreakable claim is between you and the Tracker. You're going to wait for him to arrive, and you are going to push him as far from you as you can."

"You are insane, Jaden." He had to be. "I can't push him far. A few minutes away, at best."

"You can. Push hard, and you can win us a day or two."

"I can't *do* that, Jaden. Aren't you listening?"

He ignored her protests. "What is unbreakable?"

"Jaden—"

"What is unbreakable?"

"Jad—"

"What?" he insisted.

The agreement played out in her mind, and Lara pushed the memory away as quickly as she could. She didn't want to think about Gart and his damned—

She cried out in shock. She'd done it again. Gart was on his way.

Jaden stared into the distance, his eyes focused on something far away. "It is able to be undone," he informed her. "The magic binds you loosely, because you haven't agreed to the terms your mother set. If you do, it will bind you."

He pushed to his feet and turned toward the cracking of branches.

"Magic?" He'd said that before, she was sure. *What else can I call this?* Some of the things she'd seen weren't psychic powers she'd ever heard of, and Lara had read a lot about psychic powers since she'd gotten old enough to question her own...whatever term was appropriate for her power.

Jaden didn't look at her. "Use your magic. Mean it. Try to push him a week away."

She opened her mouth to protest such an outrageous suggestion.

"You won't be able to push him that far, I'm sure, but we should test your strength."

Before she could question him, Gart vaulted from the trees, a scythe in motion toward Jaden.

It will kill him. She threw her hands out with a shout of warning. *A week! A month! The rest of my life!*

Pain sliced through Lara's head, and she screamed, pressing her hands hard to her temples.

The squeal of brakes and crash of glass wrenched her awake. Lara blinked her eyes, white knuckling the armrests as the bus skidded, tipped... For a long moment, it seemed to hover in midair. Then it thumped heavily onto all its tires and bounced.

Screams echoed off the remaining solid surfaces. In the distance, a baby cried. The tires chirped, and the bus came to a stop.

For several heartbeats, there was silence. Someone sobbed. A second joined her. A third person swore fluently. The little boy across from her let loose a piercing wail.

Lara looked to her right...then her left. Both windows were shattered. She leaned to the left, wincing at the glass shards littering the floor and the empty window frames.

Including the windshield. Isn't that supposed to be shatter-proof glass?

"Is everyone all right?" the driver bellowed. "Is anyone hurt?"

An ache in her chest drew Lara's gaze down. Her heart skipped merrily at the sight of the love bite Jaden had left on her.

"Magic," she whispered.

"Miss, are you okay?" The driver had reached her side and was looking at her anxiously.

"Fine...I think." *Anything* but *fine.*

"What in the hell happened?" the military-looking man in civilian clothing asked from behind her.

Lara winced, and the driver paled a notch.

He probably thinks I'm hurt.

"I...I dunno," the driver replied. "Maybe a baby tornado or something. Never seen anything like this before." He nodded to Lara and made his way down the aisle to check the other passengers.

Gods, just tell me no one's hurt. That's all I ask.

****

Jaden opened his eyes to the sight of Reeve and Darren hovering over him. He swallowed, wincing at his dry mouth and throat. If he was lucky, he'd have time to eat and sleep before Lara needed him again.

Thank goodness she thought her name, or I'd still be wondering what it was. A name didn't help him find her, of course, but it was something to hold tight to.

"It was her?" Darren asked.

For once, Reeve didn't bother to correct his son's poor grammar.

Jaden nodded, every muscle protesting his continued activity and lack of sleep and food. "Lara. Her name is

Lara." His muscles ached, and his eyes were clogged with grit.

Forcing the Tracker away had been a necessity. Given much more time in her dreams, Jaden would have been useless to her.

"Is she safe?" Darren persisted.

"For the moment. She can't banish him for long."

"Banish?" Reeve asked.

Jaden pasted on a weak smile. "Lara possesses the Lord's power. She is heir to the throne."

Her father's and grandfather's shock transmitted loud and clear...and their unease. Now that Jaden had confirmed it, Reeve would allow no avenue to safeguarding Lara to go untried.

Jaden's smile faded. "But she's young and untrained. We may get a day out of this move. Two at the most. I can't hope for more than that."

"Who is it?" Reeve asked. "Who am I facing?"

"We," Jaden corrected him. "He's a Tracker named Gart." He'd never heard of the Tracker, but since the mage in question was undeniably seasoned, that only meant he'd gone rogue before Jaden was old enough to remember him. *Or before I was born.*

By the stream of curses leaving Reeve's lips, Jaden guessed Gart was even more a badass than he'd originally assumed.

"Will Lara help me banish him?"

Extreme badass. If Reeve's power alone wasn't enough, Lara was in great danger.

Jared considered the question carefully. "Not yet. I haven't won her trust yet. But I have a plan to take care of Gart. It won't be easy. I'll need several mages working in unison." He met Darren's gaze. "Especially you. The Tracker has a talon in Lara. We need to sever that hold."

Darren nodded grimly. "Physically, you mean. By bringing her to Sanctum, where he cannot enter."

"No. He has a magical tie I have to sever. Bringing her to Sanctum isn't enough." *I have to win her trust. This isn't going to be easy.*

"What tie?" Reeve asked. "What has Lara agreed to?"

"Nothing, thank the Goddess, but her mother took a blood oath with Gart. She promised Lara and all she possesses to Gart as wife."

Reeve went a sickly gray color. "That means Sanctum."

"Yes. I'm afraid it does."

Darren snarled. "Not a chance. Let's hear this plan."

Chapter Four

"Miss?" A hand shook her shoulder gently. "Miss? We're here."

Lara yawned and stretched. She levered her eyes open, squinting at the motel through the darkness. She slid from the van with another yawn and stumbled toward the waiting representative from the bus company with a muttered word of thanks to the van driver.

She was second in line and weaved on her feet while she waited her turn. Whatever the woman said, it went in one ear and out the other. The only things that settled in for an extended stay were that she had up to three days of paid stay at the motel, on the bus company's bill, a continental breakfast was included in the room, and a taxi would take her to the bus station when she was ready to resume her trip.

I won't be using it. Once this hits the news, I'll have to start moving again. Part of her mind argued that she should move on now. Lara was too close to New York for safety.

Another part stubbornly insisted that she'd pushed—

Don't think about him! Lara didn't know if speaking or thinking his name worked when she was awake, but she wasn't chancing it.

I pushed him away. He was gone...for the moment. He was unable to approach her.

If Jaden is telling the truth.

Lara waffled about that for several agonizing minutes, all the while walking to her room and unlocking the door with the key the representative had given her.

The sight of the bed solidified her decision. *I'll stay the night.*

She crawled into bed without removing her shoes or jacket. Darkness took her within minutes of her head hitting the pillow.

****

Bed or no bed, Jaden needed to relieve his bladder. He opened his eyes, startling at the sight of Darren sitting in a chair he'd dragged from the main room.

Or translocated from there. It is his power, after all. Knowing Darren, he'd taken the easy way out.

"How is she?" Jaden's host asked urgently. "I know you've checked on her."

Jaden stretched, his body demanding a few more hours of sleep while he could indulge in it. But leaving Darren worrying—and his bladder aching—would be unkind and uncomfortable, respectively.

"Sleeping peacefully while the Tracker is momentarily banished from her sight. I didn't materialize for her. I just made sure she was undisturbed." He started to rise from the bed.

"Why?"

Darren's question stopped him halfway to his feet. Jaden worked at the enigmatic query, without success at understanding what he was asking. "Why what?"

"Why didn't you appear to her? You have the right to enter the dreams of your mate."

Jaden scowled. "No, Darren. I have the *ability* to do it. I do not have the *right* to. No person has the right to intrude on another uninvited."

Darren's brow creased, and he crossed his legs at the ankles. He didn't speak, as if the pronouncement confused him.

Jaden sighed. "If Lara was sure she trusted me, I would...visit, and I would ask her permission to remain within her dreams. She's not sure about me, which means I can only reveal myself to her when she asks for me. Anything else is an abuse to her, emotionally at least. If her situation wasn't so dire, I wouldn't intrude on her privacy to check on her, but it is, and so I chance that."

Lara's father seemed to consider that.

"If I force myself into her dreams, how am I better than Gart is?"

"You don't harm her," Darren murmured, seemingly lost in thought.

"Not physically, but forcing my presence on her would be an emotional assault...and at a time when Lara needs to rest to recover from physical injuries, stress, terror, anger, and sleep deprivation."

Darren paused a moment. "I think I see what you mean." But he was pensive, seemingly deeply disturbed by something Jaden couldn't even guess at.

Jaden took the opportunity to use the bathroom to relieve himself. When he returned to the bed, Darren hadn't moved a fingerwidth.

"Is there a problem, Darren?" He couldn't shake the feeling that there was.

"I never realized that humans...those raised as humans would see the use of our magic as such an intrusion. A mage raised in Sanctum would see your aid as Goddess-sent."

"You've revealed your powers to them?" If Reeve knew that, the Mage Lord would uncork worse than he had thus far.

"Just one. She's the only one I felt comfortable enough with to do so."

Jaden took a calming breath. "The one that disappeared," he guessed. "Alanna."

Darren nodded grimly. "Alanna." He paused. "Do you think that was the reason she ran from me?"

"I fear we will never know it. Lara's mother died, Darren. If it was her... You have my condolences on your loss."

The pain in his expression was stark and heartfelt, Jaden was sure. "My thanks for the news of my mate and your kind words."

Jaden tipped his head, at a loss to offer further comfort.

Darren looked around the room. "You are correct, you know."

The jump of topic was too much for Jaden. "Correct? About what?"

"Having the ability to intrude on your sleep does not give me the right to do it. My apologies." Before Jaden could reply, Darren and his favorite chair had translocated away.

Jaden shook his head in wonder and settled onto the bed again. He closed his eyes and slid back into the world of dreams.

****

Lara snapped awake, disoriented. The room took shape around her, and she relaxed.

Another day, another motel room that was little different than dozens before it.

The sun was high in the sky, and Lara checked bedside clock. Nine o'clock in the morning. She'd slept nearly fourteen hours.

Reason said she should feel rejuvenated, but Lara felt nearly as drained as she had when she'd collapsed into bed.

"You can't refuel a body like you do a car. It takes time and constant care."

Her mother had been adamant about that. She'd always insisted on proper rest and nutrition, as if there was something vital in it.

Maybe there is. As Lara fell short on sleep, got more stressed and emotionally drained, and ate less, Gart seemed to find her faster. That, in turn, led to less sleep, more stress, higher emotions, and less desire to eat. It was a vicious cycle.

If that was the case, maybe the opposite protected her from him. If Lara was rested, calm, and fed, perhaps Gart would have more trouble finding her.

And when he does, I will be rested enough to push him away again and be able to move at my leisure.

She winced at the memory of the bus accident. Thankfully, no one had been seriously injured, though she didn't doubt a few of the passengers would try to file lawsuits against the bus driver and company.

But, really, what could they complain about? According to the investigating officers, it appeared to be nothing but a freak low pressure area and one hell of a skilled driver keeping everyone safe.

I have to avoid using that particular...magic again until I learn not to wreck destruction with it. A pattern is starting to form, and a pattern will lead Gart right to me.

For now, she needed a plan.

First step...care for the body, as my mother taught me. That meant walking to the restaurant next door for a meal. That meant more sleep, after that meal.

Her scent assaulted her. *First step...a shower.*

Chapter Five

The meadow she chose to sun in was the one Jaden had taken her to the day before. The more she examined it, the more she thought she recalled having a picnic there with her mother when she was a child.

Lara blessed her lucid dreaming for allowing her to relax in such luxury.

The only niggling annoyance was the reality that she had to run in the physical world when she woke. She'd stayed in one place for well over a day. Sleep or no sleep, it was time to move on.

I need information first. Lara knew where to get that information, but still she tarried. After calling herself ten types of coward, Lara gave in.

"Jaden?" It was stupid to assume he would come anytime she called. Her heart sank in the certainty that she'd just been lucky so far.

"You need me, Lara?" He was standing a few meters away, dressed all in black, from his poet shirt to his skin-tight jeans to his knee-high boots.

Need? Lara didn't need anyone. "I had some questions."

One eyebrow arched. "You trust me to tell the truth?"

"You're planning on lying to me?" she countered.

"Not at all. I simply asked if you trust me."

"I haven't accepted your protection yet, if that's what you mean. I have questions. You're the only person I can ask. I may trust your answers. I may not, but I won't know that until I hear them. Will I?" Lara held her breath and waited for his answer.

Jaden tipped his head, apparently unconcerned that she was still wary of him. "May I sit with you while we talk?"

Lara waved him on. He crossed the distance between them, folded to the ground, and waited.

Organizing her thoughts was difficult. One question at a time. "Why can he track me in my sleep but not as well when I'm awake? Or is it not at all, while I'm awake?" She'd never been sure of that before.

Jaden didn't hesitate. "He is most likely not tracking your conscious mind at all. If he were, he wouldn't need to learn where you are from your unconscious mind."

She nodded, digesting that fact.

"Of course, we don't want to risk that. I agree that you should not spend much time in the same place, in case he is playing a game, knowing I am involved in protecting you."

"Why can he track me in my sleep at all?" She'd never heard of such a thing before.

"You erect a mental shield when you are conscious. You lack the control to erect one while you sleep."

"But you can?"

"I am a Dream-Walker. I'm stronger asleep than awake and always have been. I have been able to cast mental shields in my sleep...practically since birth."

As my mother claims I was able to move objects since birth. She'd shared stories of Lara using her powers to pull a bottle from her mother's hand to the crib when she was hungry.

When Lara didn't ask another question, he continued. "I can shield for myself and anyone that asks for my aid."

"That's how you want to protect me?"

His gaze was direct and serious. "Yes. If you allow me to."

Lara didn't answer that. She wasn't sure yet how she wanted to answer it, so it was better to focus on other questions. "When I'm tired and weak, he finds me faster." It wasn't a question precisely, but she waited to see how he'd answer it.

Jaden nodded solemnly.

"Can you teach me to shield myself in my dreams?" Her mouth went dry at the thought of trusting Jaden with such an important thing.

"That will take a lot of time, more than your banishing will win us."

"Then you won't," she guessed.

"I will, but you should ask your other questions first. The information will be more helpful to you today than fledgling lessons toward that sort of magic will be."

Lara nodded. It sounded reasonable. Now...what to ask? "What is the banishing, if it's not telekinesis?"

Jaden stretched out on the grass. "It's not telekinesis. It's magical powers. It's more than moving solid objects. Within your dreams, the Tracker has no physical form for telekinesis to move.

"You can move both physical objects and souls. In this case, you are forcing a soul a certain radius from your position and for a certain period of time. Even I can't be certain how far or long you've managed. Untrained as you are, you have little control over what you move, how far it you move it, or what direction it takes."

"Can you train me?" she cut off his lecture.

Jaden stared at her for a long moment. "Banishing is not one of my powers. It is very rare. I don't know how to do it to train you."

Disappointment and frustration warred for lead on her emotions. "Then how am I supposed to train to use it?"

"With your permission, I could bring the one other person I know capable of using this power into your dreams, but that training will take even longer than teaching you to erect a shield."

Her uncertainty was probably written clearly on her face. She wasn't sure about Jaden yet, and he was trying to talk her into bringing more people into her dreams?

He sighed. "I understand. It is far more important to get you protected. The rest can wait."

Lara rubbed a hand over her forehead. How could she know which choices were the right ones? Would bringing others into her dreams protect her better or put her at more risk?

"Protect you better," he answered her unasked question. "But you have to accept that help for it to work. Any protection is better than none at the moment."

She looked up at him, stunned by the fact that Jaden wasn't demanding anything.

"What do you know about your father and his family?"

His switch of topic left her mind rioting. *What in the world does that matter?*

****

Her cheeks darkened, making the yellow-purple bruise on her cheek fairly glow.

"It does matter, Lara."

"Not much. My mother loved him, but when she found out she was pregnant, he had some of his men pay her off to leave town. He was some sort of lord, I guess, and having a pregnant lover would have embarrassed him...socially or politically. I don't know for sure."

It took Jaden a moment to recover from the shock of that answer. "I assure you, those men were not Darren's."

Her eyes widened. "You know him?"

"Yes. I know Darren and his entire family." Hell, he'd almost ended up part of the family. *I still might, but in an unexpected way.*

Jaden pushed that thought away and continued. "Darren never did such a thing, I assure you. Neither did his parents or any other member of his family."

The pain in her expression was heart-wrenching to Jaden, and he sought to change the subject.

"Your mother... Was she Alanna?"

"I didn't know her real name until she died. She'd changed her name to Gloria as part of the...deal, before I was born. According to the pictures I've seen, she also cut her hair and dyed it to match mine...all sorts of things to make herself less recognizable."

To keep Darren from being able to translocate to her by memory. "But her name was Alanna?" he pressed. Jaden owed it to Darren to find out what had become of Alanna for him, if he could.

She nodded. "It was. Alanna Birkus."

"Then he has spent your entire life grieving the loss of her. He didn't know about you until I stumbled across you. He never knew your mother was pregnant with you. She simply...disappeared."

Her face worked its way from emotion to emotion. "If he knows about me, why isn't he here instead of you?"

Jaden sighed. She had the wrong impression again. "Dream walking isn't one of his powers. If you trusted me enough to tell me where you are, Darren and I would both be there so fast it would make your head spin."

Lara paled and shook her head.

That had been too much to hope for. Too easy.

She hurried on with her questioning. "If the men weren't my father's men or his family's men, who were they working for? Someone in his family that stood to gain by him not having a wife and child?"

"Absolutely not. I suspect they were working for the Tracker, Gart. He needed to separate you from Darren before he could form a bond with you. He had to change your mother enough to break the bond Darren had already formed with her."

She took her time answering. "Why?"

"Isolating you meant you wouldn't be trained properly, you wouldn't know enough magic to deny him, and you wouldn't be protected."

"But you're protecting me."

"If you let me."

"Why does Gart want me? What difference does—" Her face paled. "I said his name." She whispered the rest. "And I'm not strong enough to banish him again. Not yet. And...if I push him away, I'll break glass in the room, and they'll figure out it was me on the bus."

An image of the room she was currently hiding in flashed through his mind. It wasn't enough to find her with, damn it all! Why couldn't she focus on hotel stationary or something?

"Let me protect you. I give my vow that it will give me no power or claim over you."

As if challenging him, the sky clouded, announcing the Tracker's approach.

She hadn't pushed him far. Little more than a day.

Lara watched the clouds darken and roil. Lightning started arcing from cloud to cloud.

"Yes," she blurted out. "I'm asking for your protection. Don't let him touch me. Not again. Not now." *{Not ever.}*

Jaden tipped his head, biting back a smile of victory she'd surely misinterpret. Lara didn't realize what she'd done. She'd asked for his protection, but she'd asked for it in perpetuity. Unless she recanted her last request of him, he had leave to protect her as he saw fit to do so.

He let loose his power in waves, weaving the shield around them. A blinding light blazed for a moment. When it cleared, the sky was brilliant blue, dotted with white cotton ball clouds.

And we are shielded within, just as it should be.

"What did you do?" she asked.

"Extended my shield to surround us both."

"And your shield is powerful enough to..." She waved her hand in a circle.

"Gart cannot perceive us within my shield. We're safe from him."

Her cheeks darkened in a fresh blush. "Do you have to be inside the shield with me?"

"I am too young to do otherwise. If I was a decade or two older, I could make a separate shield around you. Does it bother you?"

Lara took her time answering. "No." She hurried to qualify her reply. "I can ask more questions this way."

A smile pulled up at his lips. "Of course."

For all that she'd used the questions as an excuse, Lara didn't rush to ask one. Jaden didn't rush her.

"Is it dangerous to say his name behind the shield? Can he use it to track me?"

"An excellent question," Jaden complimented her. "No. Gart cannot perceive anything that happens here."

Her expression was unreadable. "Why are you helping me?"

He opened his mouth to answer.

"The truth, Jaden. If I find out you've lied to me, I'll never forgive you." It was a solemn vow.

"It is a solemn duty to help anyone that asks me for help." It was true but not the complete truth. He prayed she'd accept it as a fact.

"But I didn't ask for your help the first time you came into my dream. I didn't even know you existed. What? You go into other people's dreams, giving them no privacy while you look around for people that need help? Not buying it."

No such luck. There is no tactful way to say this. Not before she trusts me. "I cannot enter anyone's dream without a call for help...besides my mate's. A mage always protects his mate, even when she doesn't trust him."

She swallowed hard. "That's why you proved you were real by..."

"I did ask permission to," he reminded her. "And it was one of the few pleasant ways to leave a mark on your body."

"Oh." Her expression was troubled, and she plucked at the blades of grass.

"I wanted to," he assured her. "I still want whatever intimacy you'll grant me."

Her eyes widened a bit, and her color peaked.

"Which you won't be doing anytime soon, I know. You don't know me well enough to seek that."

"Doesn't that bother you?"

He smiled. "Mate or not, I'd be surprised if you weren't wary of me."

She nodded wearily.

Jaden assessed her. "You're spending too much time in lucid dreaming." Most likely her instinct to protect herself. "My shield can protect you in a natural dream state."

Lara distanced herself from him. "Tomorrow. I'll be more vulnerable in the dream state."

It was true. *Which means she still doesn't trust me.* "What will change tomorrow?" Was she postulating she'd be more recovered and able to fight then? If she didn't indulge in a natural dream state, she wouldn't be in much better position tomorrow than she was today.

She pulled her knees toward her chest and wrapped her arms around them. "I have to move today. The bus wasn't far enough from where Gart expected to find me. I have to put distance between us, change directions, do the unexpected. I've been still too long."

There was no sense in suggesting Lara tell him where she was. She'd shied at the idea once. "I will help you as much as you let me. If you decide to trust me with your location, I promise to bring you immediately to safety."

"Is anywhere safe?"

"Yes." He didn't doubt it. If Gart was banished from Sanctum, he couldn't physically follow Lara there. He can still injure her in her dreams, though. Technically speaking, she would leave Sanctum in her dreams.

Lara stared at him for a handful of heartbeats. "I should go now."

"Travel safely." Jaden wished he could teach her spells of protection, but that required a lot of time and practice. And hands-on instruction. *What can I do for her?*

The answer was so obvious, he nearly choked when he finally locked on it. "Wait!" It was a child's magic, but it would help.

She looked back at him in surprise.

"If you find someplace to get them, find a tiger's eye pendant and a silver ring."

Lara looked down at her hand, and he noted that she already had the latter.

A discussion for later. "Gart intends to do you great harm."

"I know that," she snapped. She looked very much like Reeve when the Mage Lord was angry.

I've annoyed her. "Place sage, lavender, and sea salt in a bag and carry it on your body."

Her brow eased. "Anything else?" There was no bite of disbelief in the question.

"When you settle to sleep, light a black candle and a white one, and sprinkle sea salt and lavender under the doors and windows."

Lara nodded, seemingly deep in thought, though he wasn't picking them up.

I've been picking up a lot less of her thoughts tonight, in general. Perhaps, she was learning to build the shields on her own. Not that her juvenile attempts would be enough against Gart.

"I should go," she repeated. In the next instant, she'd disappeared into consciousness and vaulted Jaden into his own dream realm.

He lay in his dream home, smiling widely. "She's learning. She woke herself without my help or the Lord's Power, and she didn't even seem to realize she'd done it."

Chapter Six

Lara paused at the door to the shop, took a deep breath, and pushed it open. She'd never gone into a pagan shop before, but she couldn't comprehend where she'd find everything she needed elsewhere.

She already had salt, sage, and candles she'd purchased at a grocery store near the train station, but she still needed tiger's eye and lavender. That would be everything Jaden had suggested.

With Gart, everything is necessary.

She browsed along the shelves and racks, scanning the many items the shop offered. One shelf held vials of essential oils. The hooks above it held plastic sleeves of plants and flower petals.

There was lavender oil, but since she was putting the items in a bag and laying it on the floor, the dried lavender flowers seemed more prudent. Lara took down one bag, then reconsidered it. She might be on the run for quite some time. She took down all five bags of dried lavender the store had.

Sage caught her eye, and she took down a package of that as well. Though she'd purchased ground sage in the spice section of the market, that was impractical as the lavender oil would have been.

A bin of velvet and broadcloth bags caught her attention, and Lara started rifling through them. Jaden hadn't specified a color, a fabric, or a size, but the fact that there were choices meant it probably mattered.

What if I choose the wrong one? Will it still work?

"Can I help you?" a lyrical voice asked.

Lara consoled herself with the fact that the woman wouldn't think she was crazy for doing this. "I need a bag, but I don't know what color or...anything about it," she admitted.

"What sort of magic?"

"Lavender, sage, and sea salt." *I don't even know what to call it.* Her face flamed.

"Dispelling a harmful spirit? Or...cleansing a space or person?" She sounded uncertain.

"A little of both. I guess. I'm definitely dispelling or pushing away evil." How else would she describe Gart?

"How dire is it?"

"Pretty severe." Lara peeked up at her.

The other woman winced, most probably at the sight of the bruise on Lara's cheek. She pulled out a black velvet bag lined in white satin with a black ribbon tie and handed it over. "Do you have white and black candles?"

Lara nodded.

"Blessing oil?"

She shook her head.

The clerk pulled a vial of oil off the shelf and pressed it into Lara's hand. "You should use it on the candles and dab it on the bag."

Lara bit back a laugh of relief. *Jaden didn't lie to me. She knows everything he told me to do.* That was a relief.

"Do you have sea salt? Not table salt, but sea salt."

"I bought some at the store."

"May I see it? Do you have it with you?"

Lara dug the carton of salt out of her backpack and handed it to the clerk.

She shook her head. "This is processed salt. You'll want real sea salt. This way."

Lara followed her to the next aisle, where the clerk picked up a bag of salt. She handed it over, and Lara grasped a second one.

"I also need a tiger's eye pendant," Lara voiced, hoping they had those, as well.

"Come with me." She led the way to a glass cabinet and pointed out several pendants on black satin cord.

"The oval." Lara chose the largest piece.

If the other woman noticed it, she didn't comment. "Anything else?" she asked instead.

"Should there be?" Lara chanced inquiring.

"A restraining order sounds good."

"If I knew where he was, I would," she lied. Lara knew Gart wouldn't be dismissed that simply. *Besides, he has that damned claim.* Even US courts didn't always grant asylum to women forced into what they considered human rights violations.

The clerk rang up her purchases, and Lara handed over a fifty dollar bill. She placed the pendant around her throat and the rest of her purchases in her backpack.

"Rachel? How nice to have you here again. Did your brother bring you over?" a new voice asked.

Lara stiffened at the memory of the first time she'd talked to Jaden.

"Who is he, Rachel?"

Jaden called me Rachel. This woman knows Jaden.

Or Gart. Her heart stuttered at the thought that she might have blundered into a group of Gart's friends.

She bolted without looking up at the new arrival and without waiting for her change. Sounds of pursuit forced her to a desperate move.

51

Lara threw her hand out toward them and focused her magic. She allowed herself to think it, to release the power in a rush. Crashes and thumps overlapped with shouts of surprise. Glass shattered, and a potpourri of scents rose around her.

She ran the six blocks back to the train station and ducked inside. A check of the schedule showed her train would be boarding in five minutes.

They were the longest minutes of Lara's life. She expected the police to rush through the doors at any moment, looking to take her in for the destruction of the store.

Or Gart. That was enough to send shudders of revulsion down her spine.

The speakers blared out a call for her train, and Lara was the first aboard.

****

"I have no right to ask you for favors," Darren stated formally, as one would petition a stranger whose help one required.

Jared didn't open his eyes. "I cannot bring you into Lara's dreams without her permission to do so."

His ability to enter her dreams uninvited extended no further and wouldn't, even if he lived to be two centuries old or more. But Darren would know that.

Lara had refused to allow Jared to bring others into her dreams already. Until she gave that permission, it wasn't going to happen.

"I know. Enter mine and show me what my daughter looks like."

"She looks like Rachel."

"Goddess damn it, Jaden. I want to see my daughter."

The bark of order was impossible to miss. Jaden opened his eyes with a sigh, abandoning the meditation state that would keep him aware of Lara's sleep state.

Darren's expression was harsh and unforgiving.

"She looks like Rachel. So much so that I thought Lara *was* Rachel at first. That didn't last long, though. They look alike, but they act very different."

"Show me. Please...show me." His eyes pleaded for Jared's help.

He waved Darren toward the lounge opposite his own. "Meditate. That will be—"

"She's been seen," Reeve announced from the doorway.

Jaden leapt to his feet. "You're sure?"

Reeve nodded. "One of the Abberays owns a magic shop in Norfolk, Virginia. A woman she thought was Rachel came in and purchased supplies—"

"To cast a protection spell," Jaden interjected. "I told her what she needed and what to do with it, but I hadn't anticipated she'd find one of ours."

The Mage Lord nodded. "Julanne Abberay saw Lara and tried to talk to her, thinking Lara was Rachel."

"I called her Rachel," Jaden murmured. "Before I knew." His mind whirled.

"Did Julanne call her Rachel?" Darren voiced Jaden's question.

Reeve offered a terse nod. "She did, and Lara took off at a run. She used her magic to escape them. Julanne's shop is a shambles. It will take them days to clear the wreckage."

"Is she well?" Darren asked urgently.

"Skittish...and bruised. Julanne's granddaughter thought she was running from an abusive boyfriend."

"What do we do now?" Darren visibly fumed.

Jaden folded himself onto the lounge. "I wait for her to sleep and make sure Lara is well for myself."

Darren grunted his agreement and stalked away.

****

Lara stumbled into the motel room she'd engaged for the night, bypassing the bed with a sigh. She had to set up the candles and put down the salt before she allowed herself that luxury.

Her fingers shook as she anointed the length of the candles and the wicks with oil. She dragged the bed closer to the dresser and then the nightstand closer to the bed, so she could place a candle on either side of her body. Though Jaden hadn't said to do it that way, it felt right to her.

The salt lines were a little uneven, but Lara calmed herself with the fact that Jaden hadn't said they had to be. That accomplished, she settled on the mattress, tucked the bag in her bra, and lit the candles.

Lara stared at one flame and then the other. "Just keep Gart away while I sleep," she ordered.

Golden light formed an arc from one flickering candle to the other in seeming answer.

I've cast a spell. Lara didn't question it. Secure in that belief, she surrendered to sleep.

54

****

Jaden felt the call of Lara's soul in the dream realm and followed her in.

The bedroom was lush in purple and royal blue, rich textures, decadent comfort.

Surely not where she is now. From what he'd seen so far, Lara was spending what money she had modestly.

Candles burned on either side of her body, black to her left and white to her right, floating in midair, since there were no tables beside the bed. A loose shield encircled her body, drawn on the line of the candles so it surrounded the bed.

It was a masterful spell, considering her lack of training, but it wasn't sufficient to deter an elder like Gart. That a given, Jaden cast his own shield around the room.

Lara didn't respond to the change, and Jaden ambled to her side to conduct an examination of her. She was exhausted. When a person was tired enough to dream of sleeping, there could be no other explanation for it.

Jaden smiled. Finally, Lara was getting what she needed. True rest.

I should do the same. Unlike Lara, Jaden could keep his shield at full power while he indulged.

That thought in mind, he created a lounge, pillow, and blanket and settled down for the first restful sleep he'd allowed himself since he'd met Gart in Lara's nightmares.

Chapter Seven

Lara stretched, refreshed as she hadn't been in weeks. *A few more weeks of this and I might feel human again.*

The irony of that thought struck her, and she chuckled. If Jaden was telling the truth, human didn't fully describe her.

She opened her eyes, admiring the dream bedroom she'd fashioned. *I'll have to come here in dreams again.*

Her move toward sitting ended on a gasp.

Jaden was here with her, on a piece of furniture that complemented her room design perfectly. Watching him sleep seemed wrong somehow.

He watched me sleep. That thought raised the heat in her cheeks, but it wasn't in anger. Naming the emotions warring in her was impossible, so she abandoned the attempt.

Lara didn't want to consider Jaden watching her sleep as she was watching him too closely. It was intimate, and this was a man fate had apparently decreed she would be a lot more intimate with.

It wasn't hard to imagine being a hell of a lot more intimate with Jaden than they'd been when he'd left the love bite on her chest. That probably should have scared the hell out of her.

But it doesn't.

Lara folded her legs under her as Jaden often did when they sat and spoke. She did a full survey of him. His dark hair was just long enough to send wisps over his forehead and cheek.

His usual black poet shirt had been replaced with a black t-shirt that hugged the lines of his arms and chest.

A blanket covered him to the waist, and Lara practically salivated to see him without it.

Without any clothing. Now that was a mouth-watering thought.

Jaden's eyes opened, and he focused on her.

He reads my mind. Did he hear what I was thinking?

Flames of embarrassment licked up her face.

And Lara snapped awake.

She lay in her motel room bed, staring at the stained ceiling. Her body was nearly painfully aroused, her nipples hard, her slit wet and throbbing.

He heard it. I just know he did.

And, damn it, I was dressed in this night shirt in the dream. Lara didn't question that she wanted Jaden to see her in something sexy. She didn't even question why she wanted it.

Maybe hearing my thoughts is good. If he knew she was interested, he might suggest some further intimacies.

****

Jaden opened his eyes to the sight of Lara, a half-smile curving her lips, her expression dreamy, and her attention focused far away.

The smile disappeared, and she startled.

{*He reads my mind. Did he hear what I was thinking?*}

Her face and neck exploded in color, and Jaden found himself in his own dream world. The lounge and bedclothes translocated the barrier with him, because he'd created them.

It took a few muddled moments for his mind to make sense of it. When he'd accomplished it, Jaden hooked his hands under his head and smiled widely.

She was thinking about sex with me. Goddess, he wished he'd tapped into that thought as well.

At least I'm not the only one indulging in sexual fantasies. Maybe if Lara sampled enough of the fantasy variety, she might consider the real thing.

Plans to entice her warred in his mind. *I know just the thing.*

Chapter Eight

Lara retired to her motel room after an early dinner, her nerves jumping. Waking to a lucid dream state for the last few days and seeing Jaden there had wreaked havoc on her libido.

Until Jaden, I hadn't realized I had a libido.

How pathetic did that one sound? *Very,* she conceded.

Oh, sure. Lara had noticed guys and compared them to each other. And always found them lacking to some amorphous ideal.

But before Jaden, she'd never cared what kissing a man or sex with one would be like. *I've never anticipated it before.*

If it wasn't for the fact that Lara had even less interest in women than in men, she might have wondered if she was a lesbian. If she hadn't shown all the other signs of adolescence and then adulthood, she might have believed she was hormonally stunted.

She'd finally settled on the idea that she was emotionally asexual. *Until Jaden.*

Her mother had seemed worried about Lara's lack of interest in boys. And relieved at the same time.

Now—like a plant denied proper nutrition, then given a glut of it—her sexuality was blossoming. *Screw blossoming! It's growing wild.*

It seemed every unguarded moment was filled with daydreams of Jaden. The Kama Sutra and other sex manuals she'd read in her "experimental phase" had set up permanent residence in her subconscious, fueling her fantasy life with possibilities she'd once termed "silly looking."

They didn't look silly anymore. Lara could imagine Jaden's mouth between her legs, his tongue tracing the sensitive nub she'd become acquainted with in the last few days.

That thought was enough to send her to the bed. Lara peeled off her clothes and donned the silky nightgown she'd purchased at a discount shop in town.

While she'd created a comfortable dream realm bedroom, Lara was less adept at changing her attire in her lucid dreaming. Whatever she went to sleep wearing was what she was invariably wearing in the dreams.

It was a mental block, she was sure. If Lara could change her surroundings, she could surely change her clothing.

One step at a time. It had been months since she'd worn anything the least bit frivolous. This one time, she was going to indulge herself. *Completely.*

Lara climbed into bed and looked at herself in the mirror. Despite the fading bruises, she looked good: well rested, well fed, and sexy. The latter wasn't something she'd thought of herself before, but it fit, she acknowledged.

Still watching herself, Lara spread her legs and placed her fingers on the nub. Her first circle brought up a blush in her cheeks. The second enticed her nipples to harden and sent wisps of sensation to her conspicuously empty body.

The mirror was a wicked decadence, but the shabby room reflected in its depths was in stark contrast to her ideal image. *My dream room.*

I can imagine it. I can imagine a mirror in it.

Lara closed her eyes and called the layout to mind. She placed the mirror in roughly the same position it was in the physical world. Overlaying the rich colors and fabrics on the memory of the mirror image wasn't difficult, and—in moments—she was driving herself toward release, her mind providing the mirror image for her.

Oh, Mother! It was beyond good...nearly sublime.

Jaden would be sublime. Lara allowed herself to think it, secure in the knowledge that she was awake. She could say anything, think anything, imagine anything she desired, because her personal shield was firmly in place.

Visions of herself in the throes of passion alternated with visions of Jaden making a banquet of her body. Climax loomed, and Lara screamed his name, her hunger for him acute.

Movement drew her gaze to the foot of the bed. Jaden stood there, barefoot but otherwise clothed as he usually was, his expression potent.

She gasped his name, and he strode toward her, all animal grace and intent she could nearly taste.

****

"And you want me to..."

Darren's voice was drowned out by the buzzing in Jaden's ears. He shook his head, trying to clear the cobwebs from his mind. Blood rushed in his arteries, a pounding that left him feeling weak and dizzy.

Hands steadied him, and Reeve's face undulated in Jaden's swimming field of vision.

"Jaden? What is it?"

{Jaden!}

Lara's mental shout made his head ache. Blood roaring in his ears, Jaden closed his eyes and catapulted into her dream realm.

When my body crumples, Reeve and Darren will catch me.

Or he'd wake with minor injuries. That was inconsequential. His mate had summoned him into her dreams. No matter the cost, Jaden would go to her.

But the tone of her voice had been so odd. Not pained or panicked. Urgent but not afraid.

Her special room took shape around him. It took several heartbeats for her situation to gain clarity...and several more for Jaden to overcome the shock and lust clouding his mind.

Well, he overcame his shock. The lust persisted, and his cock demanded participation in the event of some sort.

A responsible voice in his mind urged Jaden to leave what was clearly a heated daydream. He sincerely doubted Lara realized what she'd done by constructing this fantasy and calling for him.

There were several highly rational reasons he wasn't going to heed that urging.

First and foremost, she'd left herself vulnerable in this semiconscious state. Not even the candle magic protected her, and Jaden could only do so if he was with her in her dream world.

That being the case, he cast his shield around the room.

Lara didn't know what danger she was in. He would have to make it clear to her, even if the shock of it cooled her blood.

Cool blood may be safest...for now. I was wrong to hint at more, considering the situation.

The last dissenting voice was less rational but no less powerful. *I want to share this moment with her. I want to see how Lara pleasures herself.*

Her head turned, and Lara stared at him. His name rasped from between trembling lips.

That was nearly his breaking point. Jaden stalked to her, torn between his duty to protect Lara from herself and his needs as a mate and a man denied too long.

He opened his mouth to speak, and Lara wrapped her arms around him and parted her lips to his. He wasn't foolhardy enough to argue that. The kiss was hot and hard. The passionate promise was a dream come true.

Literally.

Lara rearranged her legs, creating a hollow for him between her knees, and tugged Jaden toward her.

This isn't right. He extricated himself from the kiss. "I am here, Lara. This is not your dream." He had to tell her.

She moaned and tugged again. He hesitated, and Lara smiled a shy little smile. "I thought you wanted whatever intimacy I'd grant?"

"I do." *But...*

Lara reached up and slipped the spaghetti straps off her shoulders. The silky little confection she'd been wearing dipped and caught on her breasts, baring a slice of areola.

Jaden licked his lips. *We're safe here. She wants me.*

Fuck this. He captured Lara's mouth in another searing kiss, sliding his knee onto the mattress between her spread legs.

Lara lay back on the bed, and he followed her down.

****

Jaden's weight on her sent Lara's heart into overdrive. One hand closed on a strap and pulled down; the nightgown caught at her nipple, then slid away.

He was in motion, his lips trailing down her chin and then her throat. Lara arched her back, begging for him to continue by way of a moan.

He nuzzled at her nipple, his hot breath caressing her. The first suckling motion nearly brought her off the bed.

Lara tunneled her fingers in his dark hair, at a loss for any other way to urge him on. As if Jaden understood, he uncovered the other nipple and gave it the same treatment.

Pleasant shocks and tremors worked at her abdomen. Wet heat pooled inside her and spilled over.

Jaden was back at the first nipple, feasting on her as if he was starved.

I am starved. Lara pushed herself up, gasping at the bulge pressed to her thigh. She pulled up at Jaden's shirt and thrust her hands beneath it.

She tried to visualize Jaden naked, to will his shirt away. The fabric flickered...but stayed.

He released her nipple and looked up at her, his gaze intense. "Is there a problem, Lara?" he rumbled.

Her cheeks heated in a blush.

Jaden smiled. "You don't know what I look like in the nude, so you can't change my state of dress."

"Oh." Lara had hoped not to sound quite so disappointed.

"Would you like help this time?"

A lump formed in Lara's throat, and she offered a slightly manic nod.

His shirt disappeared, and Lara snapped her gaze down, drinking in every line of his chest. If knowing what Jaden looked like was important to getting him naked, she'd memorize it for future reference.

"Are you pleased with what you see?" he asked solemnly.

"Yes," she breathed. "More than anything."

"Anything?" There was a teasing tone in that question.

His meaning was impossible to miss. Lara swallowed against the growing lump. "I don't know yet, do I?" *I want to know. Now.*

Jaden nodded, then pushed himself to his knees. He took his time unfastening his jeans.

Lara watched, barely breathing. His cock was hard and red-headed, seemingly more than ready, by her uneducated estimation.

He didn't bother completely undressing. Jaden shoved the jeans to his knees and leaned over her.

He settled his hands on her thighs and pushed the nightgown to her waist. There was a torturous moment of stillness. Jaden tipped his hips, tracing the wet head of his cock along her seam.

"Yes." The plea was out in a rush of need and want.

Jaden lifted her hips slightly and thrust into her with a groan.

Sensation overwhelmed her. The stretch of her body around his length was both a delight and agony. Her muscles clenched and released, and Jaden pushed deeper.

Lara screamed. It was too much sensation, but it wasn't enough. She wanted every millimeter buried deep.

As if he heard that thought—*Maybe he did.*—Jaden pushed in until the hair at the base of his cock teased at her body.

Her breathing hitched. *More. More. More.*

Jaden drew back and thrust deeper still. Before she could react to the change, he did it again...and again. Each cycling movement of his hips was faster and more decisive.

Moans left her lips. Lara gripped his arms, gasping at the movement of his muscles beneath her fingertips.

Climax built to a razor edge and crashed over her. Jaden cursed, then buried himself to the hilt inside her.

His heat prompted a scream from her. Jaden's shout overlapped with it.

His cock bucked against her sheath, and they cried out together. In the stillness that followed, their ragged breathing was the loudest thing in the room.

Jaden lowered his weight on her and parted Lara's lips in slow, deep kisses. He smoothed her hair back from her face. One kiss led to another and a third, becoming more insistent as the heat rose between them.

Mother, we're going to make love again. Her heart pounded in excitement at the idea of it. Visions of pages in the Kama Sutra paraded through her mind. Which would Jaden choose?

He left the kiss on a groan, levering himself to his knees again with Lara still impaled on his length. The slow withdrawal prompted a gasped protest from her.

A dangerous smile curved his lips. "I was thinking something like—" The smile disappeared, and his face lost color. "You're virginal?"

His reaction made her bristle. "Excuse me?" she demanded.

Jaden peeled his gaze from his half-buried cock and focused on her eyes. "Here...in this realm, there's blood, Lara."

Her face burned. "My... I mean... Women do the first time, and I suppose my dream would include—"

"*Is* this your first time?"

His urgency raised a pit of snakes in her stomach. "Didn't I just say that?"

Jaden left her empty and aching in a rush. "You have to run. Now, Lara. Don't waste time."

"Why? I don't—"

"Because the Tracker will be closing on you fast, and he will be brutally angry at not having you first. You have to be gone before he reaches you."

"You said he couldn't see inside your shield. You did shield us before—"

"Of course!" Jaden took a calming breath. "Has Gart ever cut you in a dream? Hit you in a way that caused you to bleed in the physical world?"

67

She closed her hand on the scar that crossed her left palm, shivering at the memory. It was the one time Lara had been forced to seek medical assistance for Gart's...handling, and refusing to answer the emergency room doctors' questions hadn't been pretty.

"Lara?" he prompted her.

"Yes. A few times."

Jaden nodded. "He has limited means of tracking you in the physical realm."

"Because of my shield," she guessed.

"Yes. The blood is the single best way to track a shielded mage."

That's why he finds me faster during my period.

"Yes. It is."

Her mind spun. "If I told you where I was—"

"There may not be time. Bringing you to Sanctum and breaking Gart's claim on you is a combined effort. I don't have everyone with me we need."

"When?" The question was out before she considered the implications. *I trust Jaden. I want to be with him. Especially now.*

"Two days. Tomorrow... Allow me to bring the necessary people into your dreams and—"

"One." The idea of too many new people at once was disconcerting.

"Two," he countered. "At least two." It wasn't an order.

She nodded her agreement. "Two."

Jaden pressed a quick kiss to her forehead. "You must run. Now...wake!"

The tone of command—and probably his magic— forced her out of the dream and into the physical world.

She snapped her eyes open, sprawled on the mattress, her feet dangling over the floor.

At her first move to sit up, cramps stopped her cold. Lara scanned her gaze down her body in disbelief. The nightgown clung to her blood-soaked thighs.

Blood. He's tracking me. That was enough to propel Lara into motion.

****

Jaden opened his eyes with a deep breath, centering himself in the physical world with a prayer to the Mother Goddess, asking for Lara's protection in the days to come. His body was a riot of arousal and fear.

"What happened?" Darren demanded.

Jaden ignored the question. Even if he wanted to share the intimate details of his relationship with Lara— *And I don't!*—there was too much work to do in the next two days to waste time on something so frivolous.

"We're bringing Lara to Sanctum in two days," Jaden informed them.

"Why not now?" Her father's impatient explosion was to be expected.

Jaden opened his mouth to answer.

Reeve beat him to the punch. "That would only get her to Sanctum."

"Where she will be safe," Darren fumed.

Reeve shook his head in a negative response. "No. She'll only be safe when Gart's hold on her is broken and he is permanently banished or destroyed."

Jaden joined the discussion again. "Lara has given me permission to bring two individuals into her dreams tomorrow. We should discuss—"

"Finally. I get to meet my daughter."

Jaden hesitated, certain they were about to waste more time with an argument that could only have one resolution. "I'm sorry, Darren, but with only two... I have to prepare Lara for the battle to come. That means Reeve and Borgal. It's the only way we can keep Lara safe."

For a moment, Jaden thought he would protest the decision. *We don't have time for this.*

At last, Darren sighed and dragged a hand through his hair. "You're correct, of course."

The muscles along Jaden's shoulders eased. "Good. Then let's get everyone we need together. If Gart feels he's about to lose, he'll kill Lara to leave Reeve without an heir. Our timing has to be impeccable."

Chapter Nine

Lara paced the meadow in her dream world, dressed to run in the physical world.

Jaden had been right about Gart. According to the news reports, he'd all but destroyed the motel she'd been staying in when Jaden had ordered her to run. One person had been killed and three more injured.

Though the police had cell phone pictures and video of Gart, she sincerely doubted there was much the authorities could do against a magical Tracker.

"Lara?"

She turned and ran to Jaden blindly, throwing herself into his arms. The stress and guilt of the last day overwhelmed her, and she sobbed.

"It wasn't your fault," Jaden soothed her.

The flash of light through her closed eyelids let her know he'd shielded them from Gart.

Lara sighed, easing away from him. She opened her eyes to the sight of two more men; she stepped to Jaden's side with a gasp of shock.

Jaden steadied her, and Lara nodded. She'd told him he could bring two people with him, and he had.

He motioned to the man to his left. "This is Reeve. He is going to help you learn to use your power."

Lara surveyed him: taller than Jaden was, blond hair that reached the collar of his button-down shirt, gray at his temples, and piercing green eyes. His white suit reminded her of pictures she'd seen of the tropics. Something about him screamed that he was a man to be respected.

She nodded to him, though the urge to bow ate at her. "Thanks. I need help."

Jaden's hand movement drew her gaze to the man at his right. "And Borgal. He is going to help us spring the trap on Gart so we can shatter his magical ties to you."

The second newcomer was nearly Reeve's height, but Borgal was as dark as Reeve was light, broad as Reeve was lithe. The only similarity between them was the patches of gray streaking the hair over their ears.

While she was examining him, Borgal was examining her. At last, he offered a terse nod. "She does look like Rachel, but her essence is very different than Rachel's. And their appearances are not perfectly aligned. Her cheekbones are more defined than Rachel's are, and her eyes more pronounced. Someone who did not know them well or who was seeing them at a glance could easily mistake the two."

That freed Lara's tongue. "Who *is* Rachel?"

Reeve smiled. "My daughter. Your aunt."

Her head spun at the obvious connection. "Then...you're my grandfather?"

His bow was practiced and smooth. "It will be an honor and a pleasure to welcome you to my home."

"I imagine Darren expects his daughter to live with him," Borgal opined. "And Lara might find living in Rachel's shadow uncomfortable."

Or would Rachel find living with me uncomfortable?

Jaden didn't answer the unspoken question as he did so often. "No one makes decisions for Lara," he warned.

"Even you?" she chanced asking.

Jaden's expression was starkly serious. "You know my home is yours...when you wish it to be."

The hardening cock filling his jeans said he hoped it would be her wish soon. Borgal glanced that direction, then away, his throat moving in what was surely silent laughter.

Lara cleared her throat. "A decision for later."

Jaden tipped his head in acceptance of her non-answer.

Time to get everyone back on track. "What do we do first?"

Borgal stepped toward her. "You allow me to place a magical tag on you. That will enable me to lead the rest of the team to your location at the appropriate moment to trap Gart."

"But Gart isn't with me."

Borgal shot a look at Jaden, one heavy eyebrow raised in question.

Jaden darkened several shades. "He will be. For this to work, we have to draw Gart in."

Lara's heart pounded, and her head spun. She shook her head, a sick headache setting in.

Jaden's arms encircled her, and he drew her to his chest. "Reeve will teach you to hold Gart at bay. Borgal will make sure we reach you before Gart can harm you."

She opened her mouth to protest.

"I wouldn't suggest this if I thought you might get hurt. Do you trust me?"

Lara took a calming breath. "Yes."

Borgal dipped his head in a partial bow. "May I?"

She didn't seek guidance from Jaden. If I trust him, I have to trust the others he's brought to protect me. "Do it."

His big hands cupped the sides of her skull, and a disconcerting warmth worked inward from his palms. Moments later, he went to one knee, his head bowed deeply.

Lara shot a sideward glance at Reeve. Her grandfather's smile was strained at best.

"Explain it to her," Jaden ordered.

Borgal panned his gaze to her face. "For ten generations, my family has served the Reeves of Sanctum. I pledge my life to you, Reeve Lara, and the allegiance of my descendants."

Her mouth went dry. "But... But Reeve is a name. His name." She pointed to Reeve. "Isn't it?"

Reeve laughed heartily. "A title, actually. When I pass away, your mate will be the only person to use your given name. Everyone else will use your title, as they do with me now."

"But you're my grandfather," she protested.

He nodded, still chuckling.

"You have children," she reminded him.

Reeve tipped his head in reply.

"Why won't they be calling my father Reeve? Or Rachel?"

"The magic determines who is Reeve. You share my power, so you are the next Reeve."

That answered a large portion of her question. "What is a Reeve?"

"The ultimate protector of Sanctum."

Lara didn't know how to interpret that.

Reeve's smile dimmed a notch, and he seemed to consider his answer carefully. "You will be the leader of all the mages of Sanctum, the final word in all disputes. You alone hold the power to banish mages who pose a threat to Sanctum. Or to end their lives."

Her breathing went ragged. "*That's* my power?" *How horrible.*

"I will teach you to use it well and wisely," he promised.

"And Gart?"

His expression hardened. "My father showed him leniency. I cannot do that." One tapered hand traced the bruise on her cheek. "He has gone too far."

****

Though Lara trembled wildly and appeared faint, she nodded her agreement. "He has hurt and killed too many people." She hesitated. "What's the plan?"

Reeve motioned to Jaden, turning the discussion over to the younger man.

He didn't waste time. "You will call Gart to you in your dream state, hold him at bay with your power, and then challenge him to come to you in the physical world."

"You mean tell him where I am? You're not serious."

"Yes. I am. He will believe you have an...unrealistic expectation of your strength and will fall into the trap."

"So I'll just hang around and wait for him to show up?"

Jaden nodded.

"Who will be waiting with me?"

She won't like this. "No one."

Lara shied, and Jaden drew her close again. He winced at her shaking. "If we're there physically before he arrives, Gart will sense us, and the trap won't work."

Borgal came to his feet. "I will be listening, Reeve Lara. You won't come to harm. I vow it."

Jaden continued. "Darren will bring Reeve, Borgal, and—"

"Not me," Borgal interrupted him.

Lara pushed a trembling hand through her hair and looked ready to bolt.

Jaden glared at Borgal, forcing words through his clenched teeth. "You gave your word."

"I will be there, but not in the first wave. Reeve will hold Gart. I will come in with Rachel."

"To protect her from harm or to keep Gart busy while Rachel works?" Either way, it was a good idea.

Borgal's look was one that usually sent errant young mages scurrying. "That rogue touches my mate, and I will chop him in eighths and feed him to Louisiana gators personally."

It took a moment for the shock of that statement to wear off. When it did, Jaden smiled. "I am heartened that I wasn't similarly dispatched."

Borgal stretched his arms as if preparing for battle. "The Mage Prophet always has a plan," he dismissed that concern. "And I know Rachel. And you. You wouldn't try to lay claim to an unwilling woman."

"Rachel would never be willing for the wrong man," Jaden finished for him.

Lara grumbled something unintelligible. Her voice rose a bit. "That is one thing we have in common."

That sobered everyone at once.

****

Lara focused the rising power on the pillar Reeve was pushing toward her. Jaden had created them and given them weight.

Though she wasn't certain time passed in the dream realm as it did outside it, she'd say they'd been practicing for an hour. She was finally getting a feel for the power and how to funnel it.

"Not too much, Reeve Lara," Borgal cautioned. "Slow and steady."

Lara nodded, acutely aware of the three men training her to fight Gart.

Borgal moved, his voice passing from her left shoulder to her right. "He is old and powerful, but his powers cannot overcome yours."

That made no sense. "Of course Reeve outmatches me."

"Not Reeve. I meant that Gart cannot—"

Her power faltered in her shock. The pillar sailed toward her, and Jaden shouted out a warning. Before Lara could gather her wits to move, Borgal had a handful of her jacket. In the next heartbeat, she was pressed to the ground and covered by the bulk of his body.

The other two men rushed toward them, and Borgal pushed up and lifted Lara to her feet. In an instant, she was surrounded.

Jaden enfolded her in his arm and pulled her to his chest.

Borgal placed a hand on her shoulder. "You see, Reeve Lara. No one will harm you with us near."

Reeve nodded his agreement. "And Darren is ten times as fast."

Lara looked around at them again, noting the lack of her father's presence. Didn't he *want* to meet her?

Jaden shook his head. "You only allowed me to bring in two. Your safety demanded Reeve and Borgal, if we had to choose."

Oh... She scowled at him. "You know I hate it when you read my mind."

He smiled. "I didn't have to read your mind to know what you were thinking that time."

"Did you?" she challenged.

"No. I did not."

He sounded sincere, and she believed him. That made her regret accusing him.

Reeve sighed. "Darren was very disappointed that you only allowed two."

"Oh..." Lara bit lightly at her lower lip. She hadn't even met her father yet, and she was already disappointing him.

Jaden gave her a squeeze and released her. "You'll meet him tomorrow. For now, let's test what you've learned."

Lara took a calming breath. "Let's do this."

Chapter Ten

"Are you ready for this?" Jaden asked.

Lara turned into his arms, enjoying a moment of privacy now that Reeve and Borgal had left her dream. Jaden didn't press her for an answer to his question.

He tipped her chin up and nuzzled at her lips. Lara didn't hesitate. She'd wanted to kiss him since he showed up hours earlier.

Jaden drew away from the heat of their kiss with a growl. "We have to do this while you still have enough strength," he reminded her.

"*I* have to do it, you mean."

His hands closed over her shoulders. "Yes. You. And you will be *stunning*. Now... Are you ready?"

"Face Gart. Tell him where I am. Wait around for him to come find me," she grumbled. If someone had told her a week ago she'd agree to this, Lara would have had that person committed.

"And then we spring the trap and you're free."

"You make it sound so easy."

He sighed. "I wish I could promise you it will be. The best I can say is that everyone there will be protecting you from Gart, and there will be no lack of people protecting you."

Lara nodded. Though she'd like to argue that Borgal would be protecting Rachel, she knew his vow was sincere. He would do whatever he had to in order to protect both of them.

Still, there was something she needed to know. "You wanted Rachel. Didn't you?" Was it only how she looked that appealed to him?

Jaden's jaw tightened a notch. "There was a prophecy. It was...misinterpreted. Reeve and the other elder mages thought it meant Rachel was my mate.

"It's not so much that I wanted Rachel. She was damned infuriating, if you want to know the truth. But... I wanted a mate, a woman crafted to be perfect for me and I for her. I was blind to the fact that Rachel was the wrong woman. I believed she just hadn't grown into acceptance of the fact that she *was* that woman." He shrugged, misery etched on his features.

"She wasn't the right woman," Lara stated.

He shook his head. "In retrospect, it is so clear to me. I wanted to shake her most of the time we were close enough for me to lay hands on her. I wanted to find my mate so badly, I fooled myself into thinking Rachel was simply rebelling against the idea of being fated to anyone."

Jaden smiled faintly. "All along, she'd been rebelling against the idea of being pushed toward the wrong man. As well she should have."

"She told you that?"

His smile widened. "She didn't have to."

"I don't understand," Lara admitted.

"Have I introduced you as my mate to anyone? As Borgal announced Rachel was his own?" he countered.

She replayed their discussions with Reeve and Borgal. "No." He hadn't said anything about her being his mate.

"And I may not introduce you as my mate until you accept me as such. No matter who knows you are my mate, I may not say it in polite company until you do."

"Do you intend to accept it?"

The magar's voice echoed in Lara's mind, and her heart pounded in unease.

Jaden placed a finger against her lips and shook his head. "Not until we break Gart's hold, and not until you're certain."

She nodded solemnly. Since she wasn't certain yet, it was a good thing Jaden wasn't pressing for more.

His finger retreated, and he waited for something nameless.

At last, Lara nodded. "It's time. I know."

Jaden feathered a kiss to her forehead and stepped away. "Remember what Borgal and Reeve told you."

"No matter how powerful Gart is, my powers are superior to his." It was hard to believe, but Lara clung to it like a life ring. *It's all I have.*

Jaden didn't protest it, leaving Lara to wonder if she was shielding her thoughts, Jaden didn't want to argue it, or if he was really staying out of her head. There was really no way to be sure.

He nodded solemnly. "You will not be alone, no matter how alone you feel."

"Right."

With a wave of his hand, the sky dimmed a notch.

The shield is gone.

"I will be with you when you need me." He hesitated.

Lara knew what they both needed to believe. "I trust you."

His smile was brilliant. Then he was gone.

Though Lara knew it was a trick of the her semiconscious mind, the dream realm felt colder without him in it.

I'm wasting time. "Come here, Gart." She summoned him with an authority in her voice she didn't feel and the Lord's power she was so new to.

It took so long for his noxious presence to cast a dreary pall over the landscape, Lara had started to believe she'd subconsciously blocked the summoning with a shield.

Dark clouds rolled in, and lightning struck in the distance.

"Doesn't impress me," she muttered.

Gart strode from the trees, dark hair blowing around his angular face, his long duster flapping at his legs.

Lara forced herself not to retreat. She waited for Gart to get two body lengths from her and then ordered him to halt. To her surprise, he did.

He didn't look happy about it, but making Gart happy was decidedly not her goal. In fact, making him angry enough to make mistakes was a better plan.

Gart glared at her, his eerie flame-blue eyes assessing. "Who was he, Lara?"

Her mouth went dry. How had she forgotten that little detail would come up?

Gart continued before she could find the words to refuse him an answer. "I couldn't scent him. I couldn't find his essence. How did you hide him from me?"

Visions of Gart attacking Jaden with his scythe made her stomach churn. "Who he was is not your concern, Gart."

"You are mine, and I—"

No! "I do not accept that claim. I will never accept it, and I know for a fact that my mother's promise is not enough to bind me to you."

He shrugged as if her protest was of no consequence. "It will be enough when you agree."

"I will *never* agree," she vowed. Lara swore she could feel the tie between them loosening.

Gart clucked his tongue in censure. "You aren't hard-hearted enough to allow me to kill every person that stands between us. Eventually, you will agree. If not to save your own skin, you will do it to save others."

He really is a monster. "I don't think so," she offered coolly.

Gart took a swaggering step toward her. "This only ends one way."

"I agree."

He stepped forward again, and Lara focused her magic, pinning his feet in place. Gart shot a venomous look her way, his thigh muscles moving as if he was testing her hold.

"*This* is how it ends, Gart. I can stop you anytime I wish. The closer you get to me, the easier it will be." It was a lie, but he might think she was simply ignorant of the fact. *Please let him believe that.*

The scythe materialized in Gart's hand. "You are a child, Lara. Once I best your magic, you will be mine."

"You think so," she taunted.

Gart forced his foot a few millimeters closer to her, but his expression said it cost him in effort.

"I know it to be true," she assured him. "Here is what we are going to do, Gart. You are going to face me in the physical world, and we will see who comes out the victor."

One eyebrow went up in surprise, and he stopped struggling against her hold. "You're willing to risk that?"

A stiff smile curved her lips. "It's no risk. Smoky Mountains. Tennessee. The Midnight Cabins. Number ten. Don't keep me waiting, Gart. I know how fast you can travel, so I expect to see you today, before the sun sets. Failure to appear means you forfeit your ties on me."

His expression hardened. "If you have lied to me about where you are, you agree to be my mate."

He didn't say if I've lied to him about anything else or hidden anything from him. "Agreed. And you? If you don't agree to my terms, I will not be here when you arrive, with no penalty."

"Agreed."

He scowled. "Where is your Dream-Walker, Lara?"

She pulled her shield tighter around her, staring him down. *Not a chance. You are not hunting Jared.* "You only have one place to be, Gart. I suggest you focus on it."

He opened his mouth, no doubt to argue with her.

"You get nothing to track the Dream-Walker with, Gart. Not a thing. Think I can't recognize your kind, Tracker? Think I don't know what you need to do someone harm? The last thing I'll give you is someone else to put between us."

Lara catapulted herself out of the dream realm as Jared had taught her to do before Gart had a chance to answer. By Jared's definition, that meant she'd done the psychic equivalent of throwing ice water in Gart's face.

Good. He deserves it.

She opened her eyes to the sunlight streaming through the blinds on the cabin windows. "Today." One way or the other, it would end before the sun set today.

****

Borgal chuckled darkly, and Jared snapped his gaze to the huge Tracker.

"What is it?" he chanced asking.

"It will be *such* an honor to serve the young Reeve. She is a formidable woman."

"Is she holding Gart off well?" Reeve interrupted their discussion.

"Masterfully. She has much to learn but great power within her."

Borgal's laughter was deep and riotous. "The rogue has no idea what he's facing. She's brilliant and courageous."

Jared's question of what she was doing ended at his lips, as Borgal's eyes opened.

"She is safely awake." His smile disappeared. "Now we wait."

Darren nodded grimly. "Have everyone ready. No matter how long it takes, no one leaves until Lara is safe." He hesitated. "Considering the Tracker's age and insanity... We should have a Spell Mage and a Mage Healer here as well."

Jaden considered that. Why hadn't they realized that before? "Possibly also a Mind Healer. We will have to take certain trusted individuals into our confidence."

Reeve smiled. "I know just the ones." He guided Darren away to discuss it.

Jared started to follow them, and Borgal made a sound demanding attention. When he looked back, the Tracker had his hands folded in front of his chin, a grave expression etched on his face.

"Is there a problem, Borgal?" *There must be.*

"Your..." His gaze shifted toward Darren and back again. "The young Reeve must be removed from the battle as early as possible. I will speak to Darren about it."

He knows. They all know what Lara is to me, but propriety stays his tongue.

Jared unglued his own. "Why? If it was simply safeguarding her, you would have decided this earlier."

"Reeve Lara feels...deeply about you. Threats to you frighten her. Unnerve her."

"You think she'll endanger herself to protect me." It was a touching thought, and Jaden found it a guilty pleasure.

No! I don't want Lara endangering herself, especially not for me.

"Precisely."

Jaden found it difficult to form a response. Visions of Lara charging the scythe in a mad attempt at protecting him chilled him. "Do it. Make whatever changes you feel will protect her best."

Borgal tipped his head in acknowledgement. "Thank you for the trust you place in me. I admit I have less trust when it comes to Rachel. A failing of mine."

Hopefully, this isn't a mistake. "Perhaps it's not such a failing."

Though the entire discussion tiptoed on the edges of propriety, it was good to have someone who understood the torture of having your mate in the midst of battle with an ancient rogue.

Chapter Eleven

Lara picked at her dinner. She wasn't really hungry, but going into a confrontation with Gart depleted would be a bad idea. She'd barely touched breakfast and lunch. It was time to eat something.

Twelve hours. The waiting was nerve wracking. I should have insisted on a shorter time frame.

No. Then Gart would probably claim I'd set an unreasonable condition. Or he would have refused to agree to meet me at all...and likely tried to sneak up on me before I moved again anyway.

Though Lara didn't know the rules of engagement Gart had to follow—if any, she was fairly sure there would be loopholes he would try to use against her.

He already has. What else could you call him tricking or coercing her mother into this agreement? If Lara had shown the least bit of acceptance, he could have collected in full. *That's one hell of a loophole.*

Lara pushed her plate away. No matter how much logic there was in the idea of eating, her stomach squirmed and knotted, making the process problematic.

Not problematic. Downright impossible.

At a loss for something better to do, she started pacing.

The isolation had seemed like a good idea when she'd planned it. Isolation meant no one in the way Gart might be tempted to kill. The problem was it meant no distractions and too much time to think.

No. To obsess. Lara had spent the last twelve hours doing little else.

While common sense would dictate that her focus should be on Gart, most of her inner musings had been about Jared. Would he press for her choice as soon as Gart was dispatched? What would he do if she wasn't prepared to accept him?

More disturbing, Lara wasn't sure she wanted to refuse him. She suspected she wanted to wrap herself around Jaden and experiment with more lovemaking.

Would Jared accept that...for now?

She made another turn and stalked to the window. The sun disappeared behind the hills, painting the sky orange and pink, rays of turquoise melting into royal blue.

A knock rattled the door.

Lara winced, then turned to face it. *On the moment of the sunset. Must be Gart.*

As if in answer, the man in question called out her name.

"Come in, Gart. It's open." *Why would I lock it? He'd just break it down. And it would only delay the end.*

There was a moment of seeming hesitation. Then the knob turned and the door swung inward.

The sight of him was somewhat shocking. His hair had been tamed into dark curls shot with threads of gray. He was clean-shaven. Moreover, Gart's rough clothing had been replaced by clean, pressed evening wear. He wore spit-shined knee-high boots and a gentleman's evening coat.

A smile curved his lips. "I take it my appearance is pleasing to you."

He's counting on it. "It might have been once. Now I know the wolf hiding in the wool and silk. It ruins the effect."

His smile faded, and the muscle at the back of his jaw twitched. His step into the room was definitive, and when he swung it shut, the door banged against the frame and rebounded a few inches.

"Tell me why," she demanded.

Gart went still and stared at her.

"Before we try to tear each other to pieces, tell me why you've done this. Why me? Why this?"

He sighed. "It is a very long, tired story about a family, a place, and a woman." Gart took another step toward her.

Lara raised her hand, palm out, in preparation to use her magic. "The short version. Indulge me. I think I deserve that much."

He scowled, then nodded. "Long before your grandfather's time, there was an epidemic. A plague brought to Sanctum from the human realm by a...dallying mage. It killed many of our kind before the mage healers happened upon a spell to cure it and another to prevent it. By that time, my mate—and the Reeve's as well, had perished. Children were especially susceptible, and we found ourselves with few young to continue into the future."

He paused and Lara nodded.

"Eviana's mate had also died in the epidemic. She loved me. We weren't mates, but it was the only thing left to us."

So sad.

It doesn't excuse him, she hastened to add.

"The Reeve wanted her as well. He insisted." Gart's expression went sour. "He said the perpetuation of *his* line was more important than the perpetuation of mine.

"When I refused to cede to him, he banished me from Sanctum. I lost everything because of him."

"And how do I feature into all of this? I hadn't even been born yet." *The agreement with my mother was signed at my birth. There is no way he could have known what I'd look like as an adult, so it can't be that I resemble Eviana.*

"When you are Reeve, you can undo what was done to me."

"You could have simply asked for that. You could have asked the current Reeve for it." Reeve struck her as a compassionate man. Surely he would have allowed Gart to return.

He shook his head, the muscle in his jaw twitching again. "This way, it cannot be undone at a Reeve's whim."

"After the crimes of you killing and harming innocent people, it can't be—"

"I did what I had to do," he insisted.

"You believe that, I'm sure."

His expression promised pain for challenging him. "Let us end this. I grow weary of the hunt." The scythe appeared in his hand.

Before Lara could rally her magic, three male bodies appeared between them with a rush of displaced air. The center one turned, ducked between the other two, and lunged for her.

Her scream of shock started when his hands closed on her arms and ended in a strange—and very frilly—bedroom.

Lara looked up into deep blue eyes that closely matched her own. His hair was dark waves of gold around a pale, strained face, but he appeared no older than she was. Surely this wasn't her father.

"So like your mother," he breathed.

He must be my father. Lara had never seen him before. Her mother hadn't even had pictures of him to share. *Probably so I wouldn't go looking for him. Would my magic have allowed me to find him if I knew more about him?* That was likely, and so Gart wouldn't have wanted her able to try.

"Darren!" another man barked.

Her father leaned down and planted a quick kiss on Lara's forehead. "Stay here. You will be protected."

One swish of air punctuated his move across the room. A second heralded her father and two other people disappearing.

She recognized Borgal as one of the two. It took a moment for the fact that the other was her exact double—down to the clothes they were wearing—to strike Lara fully. *That must be Rachel.*

The room wasn't empty. Three women stood against the far wall, their hands clasped and heads bowed to her. They were her protection?

They do have magic, and unlike me, they're trained to use it.

"Welcome, Reeve Lara," one of them stated. She raised her head and motioned to a plush chair. "If we may?"

91

"I don't understand," Lara admitted. May they what?

The woman smiled, and her green eyes lit in amusement. "We are here to heal and comfort you."

"I thought you were here to protect me."

"That as well, should it become necessary."

Lara made her way to the chair on shaking legs, her mind in a riot. She replayed the last moments with Gart over and over.

The certainty that one of the first men Darren had brought in was Jared turned her stomach to ice. Gart knew what Jared looked like from the dreams. He already wanted to do Jared harm. What would stop him from doing it?

"Shhh. Be at rest, Reeve Lara."

The youngest of the three women ran her fingertips along Lara's forehead, and Lara let her eyes slip shut. At the second touch, exhaustion seemed to weigh her down.

****

Jared had barely righted his senses after the translocation when the Tracker's roar announced that Lara and Darren were safely away.

Good. There is no chance of Gart using his scythe on her.

"I should have known. The little Dream-Walker. You have no business in this realm, boy."

Jared opened his mouth to reply.

"*I* do," Reeve interjected coolly.

"I had an agreement with your heir," Gart countered. "She is in breach of—"

"Not at all. She promised to be here when you arrived. She was. There is no breach. As for her absence now? The Reeve protects *all* his people. It was my determination that Lara required my protection from you. I ordered her removal from a dangerous situation."

Gart sneered and raked his gaze up and down Reeve's body. "So like your father. Proud and selfish. The heirs of Reeve are more important than any other."

A rush of air and the tang of magic announced Darren's return. Borgal appeared at Jared's side, his scythe in hand. Darren lighted just behind Reeve's Tracker, and the heat at Jared's back was undoubtedly Rachel.

Borgal's voice was low in warning. "As if your own heirs were of any importance to you?"

Gart paused a moment, his expression broadcasting his calculation. "You are a Tracker. Of whose line?"

Borgal cut off Reeve's answer before the first few sounds had emerged. It was an incredibly bold and rude move. Reeling in surprise, Jared had to work at comprehending Borgal's answer.

"Reeve Adrien gave you the choice of taking your own heir with you. As I have heard the tale, you refused. Did you ever wonder what became of your son?"

Gart didn't reply. His expression didn't soften.

Reeve broke the moment by inserting his answer. "My father and mother raised Borgal as my elder brother in name. Your heirs resumed their rightful place as the personal Trackers to the Reeve." He didn't need to state the obvious. Gart had broken with his family's blood vows when he'd crossed Reeve Adrien. He had abandoned his honor.

"Slaves to the spoiled Reeves," Gart accused. He shot a look that promised death at Borgal.

Rachel shifted, and Gart's eyes narrowed.

"I was promised the girl. Whatever your lap dogs did to her in the few moments she was gone, she is still mine."

"You cannot have her," Jaden snapped. It surprised him that Borgal hadn't offered his own protest, since it was clear Gart thought Rachel was Lara. *That is the plan...for now. Perhaps Borgal is controlling his instincts to preserve the plan.*

"It is not your place to refuse me, Dream-Walker."

Rachel wrapped her arms around Jared's chest and pressed to his back. His heart stuttered, and he glanced at Borgal out of the corner of his eye. The Tracker wasn't reacting, though it had to boil his blood to see Rachel wrapped around Jaden this way.

This is taking the pretense that Rachel is Lara too far.

Rachel's voice was firm and clear. "I say it is."

Gart's gaze narrowed, murder burning in his eyes.

Jared shot a questioning look at Borgal, but the younger Tracker was unreadable. *How much has he changed the plan? Why didn't he warn me this was coming?*

A worse possibility flitted in his mind. What if Borgal was working with his father?

Gart shot for Jared with a bellow of rage. Rachel fled for her father's back.

"Now, Reeve Lara," Borgal ordered.

It's not Rachel. For some reason, Borgal brought Lara back here. Jared fought for the words to protest this insanity.

94

The scythe swung in a deadly arc. Lara's power shoved Jared into Darren's grip.

In a whirlwind of moving air, he and Darren landed in Rachel's bedroom. They sprawled in a heap on the plush rug.

Jared's move to throttle Darren for taking Lara back and leaving her there ended at the crush of a woman's body against his side. Her lips pressed to his, and Jaden moaned Lara's name.

Darren transported away without them, and Jaden thumped to the rug where Darren's thigh had so recently supported him. He stared up at Lara in disbelief.

****

The healing of Lara's many wounds passed in a pleasant haze of warmth and whispers. The women's combined touch was soothing, both mentally and physically.

But relaxing in these strange surroundings wasn't in the cards. Lara's nerves jumped and shimmied. Something was wrong. She could practically taste it.

"Reeve Lara?" one of the older women inquired.

{Remember what I told you, Reeve Lara.} Borgal's voice was faint, but Lara didn't doubt it was real.

What did he tell me?

"Reeve Lara?"

"Wait."

The room went silent.

Lara searched her memories of Borgal's instruction of her. There weren't many.

I'm not facing Gart now, so whose power is stronger doesn't matter. I'm not using my power, so using it in a steady stream doesn't matter.

What else was there?

The memory was slow coming, but she didn't question that she'd found the right one.

"You can draw people or objects to you, as well as push them away, but only if there are no obstacles between you. Except for Transporters like your father. If you call a Transporter to you, he can transport to your side with anything...or anyone he's holding."

That was it. It had to be it.

What or who do I need to transport? She hoped it wasn't Gart. Though she imagined the magic that banished him from Sanctum would injure him, she didn't want to bring him here to prove it.

There was no answer. Lara closed her eyes and tried to picture the cabin she'd vacated. The indistinct memories came into sharp focus.

Gart thundered toward Jaden, his scythe raised. Her heart skipped a beat in the certainty that this was really happening.

{Now, Reeve Lara.}

What she guessed was Borgal's gaze shifted from Jaden to Darren and back again. Using it as orientation, Lara focused her power on shoving Jaden toward Darren, then summoning them both to her.

The magic had never felt so concrete before. A thump shook the floor, and a whoof of air left someone's lungs.

Lara hesitated to open her eyes. What if something went wrong?

At last, she couldn't stand not knowing. She opened her eyes, letting out her breath in a rush at the sight of Jaden reaching for her father.

She lunged out of the chair, and the thick, cream-colored carpet cushioned her knees. Jaden turned toward her, and Lara kissed him, desperate to show her gratitude that he was still alive.

Something indistinct rumbled between their mouths, and Jaden took the lead, threading his fingers through her hair.

Air rushed past her cheek, and Jaden's mouth parted from hers. Lara opened her eyes, and they stared at each other for a long moment.

He trailed his fingertips from her scalp to her cheek. "You didn't come back. It was Rachel after all." His voice held a note of awe.

"Of course not. You all said—"

Jaden levered himself up and parted Lara's lips in a kiss.

"Reeve Lara? You should clear space for when they return," one of the women with her instructed.

Lara broke away from the kiss with a sigh. She pushed to her feet, and Jaden did the same.

His arm encircled her waist, and Jaden led her toward the chair she'd vacated. Lara nudged him toward the matching love seat instead; he didn't hesitate, and they settled into it together.

Though Lara couldn't think of anything to say, the intimacy of the moment was a comfort. Long minutes passed in near silence.

"How long will they be?" Lara asked.

Jaden's shoulder moved in a shrug. "Since the plan has changed, I can't begin to guess."

Her answer melted into a gasp, and her heart went wild. Lara pitched forward onto her hands and knees, an unreasoning need to escape the sensation driving her.

The room erupted in movement, and voices overlapped.

"Calm, Reeve Lara."

"She cannot. This is not her doing."

"Her heart is failing her, but I cannot find a physical fault."

"Can your force it to beat normally?" Jaden pleaded.

"No. This assault is magical in nature. The spell must be broken."

****

Jaden stared at Mirica in disbelief. *The rogue is attacking Lara. Why did we believe bringing her here would shield her from him?* "Can it be undone?"

"Get her to the bed."

He scooped Lara up and accomplished the task, his emotions rioting. "We have to contact Darren." Why hadn't they considered having another Transporter or someone capable of communicating between the two groups to handle this?

"He cannot do anything for her," Avelia corrected him.

"He could take me there, so I can beat Gart until he—"

"D-dead," Lara stuttered out. She licked her lips. "H-he's d-dead."

98

"It's what humans call a booby trap," Mirica offered. "He must have set it when Reeve Lara was very young. An infant, perhaps."

"If he dies, Lara dies with him?" Jaden guessed.

The Spell Mage nodded in response.

"What can we do? We have to do *something*." *It can't be hopeless.*

Mirica placed her hands on Lara's chest and closed her eyes.

She's using her magic to unbind the spell. As a Spell Mage, divining what spell had been used and reversing it was her gift.

Lara's labored breathing deteriorated, and her lips took on a purple hue. Jaden's heart stuttered at the sight of it.

"Ask her, Jaden," Mirica ordered.

"Ask her what?"

She turned her eerie lavender eyes on him. "You know what you need to ask your mate."

Avelia gasped, and her face went crimson. She averted her gaze.

Jaden stared at Mirica, shocked at the presumption of ordering such a thing. The Spell Mage continued before he could protest.

"The rogue's plan was to make this unbreakable. He had created a hollow that once contained the tether binding them. It is unnatural...an affront to Reeve Lara's system. The only way to end the assault is to fill the hollow with another attachment."

His head spinning, Jaden nodded.

"He didn't believe her mate would be with Reeve Lara when the trap sprung on her."

"And that would have killed her." Jaden didn't question it.

"Hurry," Avelia urged him. As a Mage Healer, she would know Lara's physical state intimately.

She's slipping. Jaden eased Lara into his arms, his heart aching at what he was about to do.

"I didn't want to do it this way," he breathed.

Just do it before she's incapable of answering. "Accept me as your mate, Lara. Please. I need you with me." The fact that Sanctum needed her was immaterial. He had set into this for personal reasons, and that hadn't changed.

Her eyes opened, and Lara shot him an unreadable look.

Jaden smoothed her hair, at a loss. "Do we need to consummate immediately?" he asked Mirica.

"No. Just bind the promise."

"Good. I will give you all the time you need, Lara. You are obligated to nothing but the acknowledgment that we are mates."

She didn't answer.

Panic drove him on. If Lara didn't accept before she lost consciousness, she would die.

Jaden pulled her fully into his arms, his breathing hitching. "Save yourself, Lara. Please. If you leave me, I have nothing. You are everything to me. Refuse to consummate if you wish, but refuse later. Refuse to be mine. If you live, I can console myself with the fact that—"

"I accept."

Her answer was so low, Jaden wasn't certain anyone else heard it.

They don't have to hear it.

A gasp from Mirica proved that thought in error. "Finish it quickly," she urged him.

He eased Lara back slightly. "You are my mate, Lara. I accept you, good and bad, for all eternity. I will be by your side in this life and the next, your lover and your helpmate."

Jaden feathered his lips against hers, and Lara sucked in a deep breath. She laid a kiss on his chin, then collapsed against Jaden's chest.

His heart stampeded in the certainty that he'd been too slow. Lara moved, and he released a breath he hadn't realized he'd been holding.

Avelia nodded shakily, and Mirica sank to her knees beside the bed, looking spent.

"I'm so tired." Lara's voice was raw and weak.

"Sleep," Jaden offered. "We are here to protect you."

Her head dropped back, and Lara gave in to the need. Jaden settled her to the mattress and pressed his lips to her forehead.

The wash of magic and air heralded Darren's return. A feminine snort confirmed Rachel was with him.

"It is a good thing I don't sleep in that bed anymore," she opined. "As it is, I think this visual has scarred me for life."

Jaden didn't bother to answer her.

"Is Lara well?" Darren asked urgently.

Mirica answered for the group. "The spell the rogue set has been...forestalled."

Forestalled. Not undone. If I die, it will finish the job. Lara cannot live without me in her life...unless Mirica can unravel the spell later.

Avelia took over. "Sleep will set her right now."

Darren breathed a sigh of relief. "Good. I have to go back now." He transported out without waiting for a response.

"You should sleep too, Jaden," Avelia counseled. "You have pushed yourself too hard of late."

"It was necessary," he defended himself.

"But over now."

Jaden glanced up at Rachel. "Do you mind?" he asked.

She smiled, seemingly much more at ease now that she had her mate. "I don't sleep here anymore. She's welcome to this room and anything in it."

A smile pulled up at his lips. "The dresses you hate?" Rachel had loathed ceremonial dresses from the time she was old enough to voice complaints about them.

Rachel didn't confirm it. Or deny it. One tapered brow went up, and she smirked at him. "You'll make a good mate, Jaden. I wanted to tell you that."

"Just not your mate," he countered.

"Yes. Not mine." Rachel hesitated, then waved the other women toward the hallway. "Privacy. They need sleep. You can watch over Reeve Lara from the adjoining room."

No one argued with her. In moments, the bedroom was cleared. Rachel dimmed the light on her way out and shut the door behind her.

Jaden stretched out beside Lara, enjoying her heat against his skin. He thought he was too keyed up to sleep, but within minutes, he was proven wrong.

Chapter Twelve

Lara drifted into the light dream realm she shared with Jaden. It was no surprise that he was there moments after she arrived, seemingly asleep but drawn into her dream nonetheless.

Jaden hadn't appeared on the lounge he'd created the other times he'd come to her dream bedroom. Instead, he was sprawled on the bed beside her, his curved fingers snug to her waist in his sleep.

She savored every nuance. Laying here with Jaden, it felt as if she'd spent the last few days wasting opportunities.

I have wasted them. How long had she denied her attraction to Jaden?

Too long.

And now we're mated.

It hadn't been difficult to accept Jaden, and not just to save her own life. Hearing him say her living would be enough for him had been incredibly touching.

And arousing. Had she not been exhausted, Lara would have been all over Jaden, stripping off his clothing, their audience be damned.

We haven't consummated yet. Lara stared at Jaden, replaying the discussion in her memory. He'd said they weren't really mates until they consummated.

But we could be. Jaden had left that final step to Lara.

She didn't waste time arguing the situation. Lara focused on her clothing, using the dream state to shed it.

****

The body nestling to his was undeniably Lara. Her lips pressed to his, and Jaden parted his, urging hers wider for something intensely carnal.

Lara didn't disappoint. Their bodies entwined, and hands started to roam.

Jaden groaned at her state of undress. He didn't question what she wanted; his sleep pants were gone in an instant.

As if taking that as an invitation, Lara straddled him. The wet heat of her slit against his cockhead taunted him. Before he could thrust up, she moved, taking him in.

The rest passed in the sweet rush of moving bodies. Their shared climax was potent, drugging Jaden's senses with the rightness of it all.

Lara sank to his chest, her back rising and falling smoothly beneath his hand. A chuckle rumbled against his throat.

Jaden smiled. "And what is so amusing?"

The kiss pressed to his jawline made Jaden shiver in delight.

"I suppose you'll be calling me your mate now."

"You did agree to acknowledge it," he replied.

"And we consummated."

The smile drained from Jaden's face.

Lara went still, then raised her head. "What did I say wrong?"

"We haven't...precisely—"

Her hand motioned up and down their still-locked bodies. "What do you call this?"

He winced. "It has to be in the physical world." Something told Jaden he'd be waiting a long time for that consummation now.

Her brow furrowed in what was surely confusion.

"Lara—"

"Wait a minute."

Jaden snapped his mouth shut hard enough to clack teeth.

"What happens here affects the physical world." Lara rushed on before he could reply. "It can leave bruises and make me bleed."

He nodded.

"Then why is it different?"

"Will you be angry if I tell you I've never understood it, either? I don't know why it matters. You can't conceive a child in a dream walk. Perhaps that is the difference. Or perhaps it has to do with the sharing of physical forms specifically."

Her answer was slow coming. "I guess I can't fault what you don't know."

"We can ask Miriza," he suggested.

"Who is Miriza?"

Jaden twisted a lock of her golden hair around his fingertip. "She's what we call a Spell Mage. Since the mating ritual is essentially a spell, she should know why it makes a difference."

"Because she knows the spell?"

"Because her power centers around making new spells and dissecting the spells of others to undo them." He paused for a moment. "She's the one who saved your life last night."

Lara shook her head. "You did that."

"Mirica told me how. I never would have guessed the solution she proposed. I wouldn't have even known what the problem was in time to save you without her."

She was silent for a long moment.

She's thinking about dying. Left to me alone, Lara would have died.

"Then how do you know it doesn't work in a dream."

"We call this a dream walk," he corrected her.

Lara stared at him.

"Other Spell Mages have told us it's impossible."

"Then...you really don't know for sure."

Jaden's face flamed in embarrassment. "I guess not," he admitted. "We've never had reason to mistrust their determination."

"Better safe than sorry then."

"Beg your pardon?" *What in holy Sanctum did she mean by that?*

"We should consummate in the physical world. Just to be sure."

Jaden didn't question her intent. He eased them out of the dream realm, his physical body more than ready to oblige her.

Lara went to work on his shirt, dragging the tucked tails out of his jeans, then pulling the buttons on his jeans open. Their mouths meshed.

"You are not alone," Darren informed them, his voice gruff.

They startled out of the kiss and turned their heads toward Lara's father nearly in unison.

****

Lara swallowed the lump in her throat, butterflies staging a revolt in her stomach. "We didn't know."

"Most people don't expect to wake with an unexpected guest in their bedroom," Jaden added. "I have explained that to you, Darren."

Her father screwed up a scowl.

"Do not question my intentions," Jaden continued.

"I didn't plan on it," he huffed. "But Reeve wants to see you as soon as you wake. You have awakened." He looked at Lara, his expression softening.

She nodded solemnly. Darren wanted to speak to her. That much was clear.

Jaden sighed. "We should bathe and dress." Though his tone hadn't changed overmuch, his meaning was impossible to miss.

Her father stood and smoothed the front of his faded jeans. "That won't be necessary. There are others waiting to eat. You will cause delay for everyone if you tarry that long."

Jaden flopped to his back on the abandoned pillow, grumbling something Lara didn't catch.

Her father's tensing muscles warned that it wasn't an invitation they might decline.

"We'll be right down," Lara hastened to assure him. "I have to use the toilet first." *And at least splash water on my face and wash my hands.*

Darren smiled. "Of course. There is a set of toilette in there for you."

"But...my bag?" They hadn't left her belongings behind, had they?

The hurt in his expression said she'd asked the wrong question. He motioned his hand in an awkward and falsely casual way. "If you wish."

"You chose the others," she guessed.

"A trinket or two," he dismissed her.

"Then I'd like to use them."

A weak shadow of a smile curved the edges of his lips. He offered a quick bow of his head. "I will see you downstairs."

In the blink of an eye, he was gone...popped away to wherever he'd decided to go.

"I will never get used to that," Lara complained.

Jaden laughed. "You will. Much faster than you might believe." He fastened his jeans, pushed up from the bed, and offered Lara his hand. "Shall we?"

As if in answer, her stomach grumbled.

****

The dining room was full of people, and all of them stopped conversing to stare at Lara. She looked down at her rumpled clothing, well aware that she looked like a pauper entering the lap of luxury.

At least my hair and teeth are brushed and my face and hands are washed. But still, she'd been in her clothes for a full day.

Jaden placed a hand on her lower back and leaned toward Lara as if to whisper something. What came out of his mouth was nothing resembling a whisper, and Lara cringed.

"It's Darren's fault...and Reeve's. They are the ones who didn't allow us to bathe and dress."

Lara swallowed down a laugh, mindful that she didn't want to offend her newfound family. Both men darkened in a blush, and the others snickered, laughed, or hid what she would assume was smiles behind demure hand gestures.

That was her breaking point. Lara laughed at everyone's reactions more than at Jaden's ridiculous accusation. It felt good to laugh.

Reeve cleared his throat and motioned Lara to the table. Jaden took her elbow and guided her to Reeve's side. Every man in the room, save Reeve himself, moved to seat her. Her father beat the others to the honor.

Lara's head spun lightly at the turn of events.

"Is there a problem, Lara?" Reeve shifted in his chair, giving her his full attention.

"Not really." She hesitated. "I've just been on the run so long..."

"You haven't been treated as you should have been."

"I've never been treated like this. I feel like a princess." Lara scowled down at her clothes. "I don't look or smell like one, I know."

Jaden took the chair to her right, and the others moved to sit. Darren took the seat across from her. The women who'd taken care of her the night before were on Jaden's side of the table. She didn't recognize any of the others.

"You forget The Princess and the Pea," Jaden reminded her. "Princesses don't always look the part."

"I suppose that's true enough."

"You will after today," Reeve decreed.

Lara's heart skipped merrily. "Meaning what?"

Reeve's hand arced in an encompassing motion. "Adara will tend to your beauty and hair needs."

The woman to Darren's left tipped her head. "You have a natural beauty, Reeve Lara. Unless you wish changes to your hair, there is little I can do to enhance you."

Lara smiled. "No one has ever called me a natural beauty before."

Adara waved off the statement as one would a pesky insect.

Reeve motioned down the line. "Jules and Tricia will handle your wardrobe."

Jaden cut in. "Rachel has already given Lara all the clothing left in her room."

"I should thank her." Lara made a mental note to do that when she saw Rachel next.

Tricia—Lara guessed that Reeve had introduced them in order—made a sour face. "Most of Rachel's clothing will be completely unsuitable for Reeve Lara."

"Why?" The question was out before Lara could stop herself. Her face burned in embarrassment. "I mean... It looked to me like Rachel is the same size as I am."

Jules smiled a secretive little grin. "In bodily dimensions, she is, but your character is very different. A true artist matches clothing to individual."

Adara nodded emphatically. "I would hardly choose the same hairstyles and cosmetics for the two."

Lara shook her head in confusion. "But the clothing she was wearing when—" Realization struck her hard. "How could she have been wearing the precise clothing I was?"

Reeve answered for her. "Borgal arranged it. We had to trick Gart into believing Rachel was you."

"Okay. I buy that. Then... How are Rachel and I so different?"

Tricia and Jules smiled at each other and then at Lara. "I believe you will find that you are when you come to know Rachel better."

Tricia bounced up from the table. "I believe I will sort the clothing Rachel left behind while you eat. It will save us time later."

Jules followed in her wake. "Most definitely."

"But your breakfast?" Lara called after thcm.

"One never eats when the muse is upon her, young Reeve," Jules sing-songed back.

Adara rushed to join them. "I should do the same with the toiletries." She tipped a head to Lara. "I will see you shortly, Reeve Lara."

"Please don't take any of the ones my father got for me," Lara called after her.

Adara chuckled and stopped to shoot Darren a mischievous look.

Darren went a stunning shade of red. After a moment, her father offered Lara a sheepish grin. "I...asked Adara to help me choose something that would complement your essence. While you slept this morning. I had chosen the brushes and such. She helped me choose the scents."

"Oh... Thank you both."

Adara smiled widely and turned toward the foyer again. All three women were gone in a flash, leaving Lara stunned at their abrupt departure.

Reeve continued as if there had been no interruption. "Hess and Nelson will be your personal guards."

The two men at the opposite end of the table offered a salute of only the index finger, the thumb and other fingers folded together into an o. She suspected it was ceremonial.

"What about Borgal?" she asked Reeve. Wasn't he her bodyguard?

Jaden answered. "Borgal will act as guard if he is already in your proximity, of course. Otherwise, he will let Hess and Nelson know if you require their assistance."

Lara's stomach clenched. "So he's watching what I do all the time?"

"No!" Darren protested. "Nothing like that. He watched you yesterday, but usually..." He glanced at Reeve, seemingly at a loss to explain it.

"The humans have...alarms. A signal sets off a noise that those who protect can hear?" Reeve asked.

Lara nodded. "So... Borgal only watches when something sets off that alarm?"

Reeve's face smoothed. "Yes. Precisely."

"I see. I guess that's all right then."

He went on, motioning to the three women on the same side of the table as she and Jared occupied. "You met Avelia, Mirica, and Juniatta last night."

"Not formally," Lara interjected. "I know Mirica is... Jaden called her a Spell Mage. Avelia is a doctor."

"Mage Healer," the woman in question offered gentle correction.

"Mage Healer. What is Juniatta's magic?"

Lara focused on the woman just in time to see her avert her gaze. A sideward glance answered what Juniatta had been looking at. *Darren.*

"I am a Mind Healer, young Reeve." She made a hand motion that made no sense to Lara. "After your ordeal, Jaden and Reeve felt you might require...comforting."

"You're the one who calmed me down when I was left here."

She nodded and smiled.

"They are here to check for lasting damage and spells that might need attended to," Reeve informed her. "They can certainly do that while we eat."

With a wave of her grandfather's hand, plates appeared on the table. Lara's plates had more food on them than she could eat in three breakfasts. Mugs of coffee, various teas, and hot chocolate were crowded between glasses of various juices, milk—white and chocolate—and water with lemon.

A glance around showed the other plates were more modestly apportioned. Lara peeked up at Reeve, at a loss to interpret it. Did they think she was starving?

He laughed. "I forget sometimes that you didn't grow up in a magical household."

"I don't understand." Lara hastened to admit it; she would never learn if she didn't question the things she didn't understand.

Jaden took over the explanation. "When we feed children or when we have a dinner party with a set menu, we usually set the spell to supply particular foods and amounts. For adults in a family—or in an informal gathering of friends—the spell is set to provide whatever the individual wants to eat."

Lara glanced down at her plate. "I didn't envision enough food for three or four people. I'm hungry, not starving."

He shook his head, his throat bobbing in what she suspected was laughter. "No. Those would be all the possible menus for breakfast that flitted through your mind when Reeve said we were ready to eat."

"So you focus only on what you want to eat that meal?"

"We can try it at lunch. For now, eat what appeals to you."

"And eat well, Reeve Lara." Avelia pulled out her doctor—Mage Healer—voice. "You have not done so of late." She tipped her head to one side, assessing. "Yes. I will be ordering a few healthy additions to your meals this week." That decided, Avelia picked up her fork and started eating her fruit plate.

"Why do I get the feeling I've lost control of my life?" Lara muttered.

Juniatta laughed around a mouthful of food, swallowed, and smiled. "Not at all. You'll find the orders will be to your tastes. The last thing a Mage Healer or Mind Healer wants to do is stress a patient. Finding a palatable way to treat patients is one of the many benefits of using magic."

The rest of breakfast passed in amicable silence.

Halfway through the omelet, Lara suspected vegetables appeared in the layer of cheese and sausage. She slid a glance at Avelia, but there was no way to know for sure if she'd just had her choices overruled.

The addition was tasty, so Lara decided to let it slide.

Chapter Thirteen

At the end of breakfast, Jaden's plan to whisk Lara to a bath was short-circuited. Then again, so was Darren's plan to sit down and talk to her. Jaden shot Darren a weary look.

Jules shooed them away. "Go on now. I'm certain you each have things to do."

Jaden couldn't conceive of anything he wanted to do more than consummating his mating with Lara.

As if she heard the complaint, Tricia took Jaden by the arm and led him toward the front door. She kept her voice low. "You have plans, Jaden. I know you do, but would you dishonor your mate by not offering her the traditional sign of your intentions?"

He was about to protest that he already had a promise necklace. Realization stilled his tongue, and he nodded his agreement. He had a promise necklace, but it was one that had been chosen with Rachel in mind and carried her essence from decades of wear. It would be an insult to offer that to Lara.

She nudged him away, and he started for the marketplace. A glance down at himself, had Jaden reversing course. He should at least indulge in a quick shower and a change of clothing before going to the shops.

In his bedroom, he started stripping off his clothing. The bedroom resonated with him, and Jaden considered it. He looked around the room, making plans he hoped would please his mate.

My mate. How long had he been frustrated by the idea that he would never get to enjoy that phrase? *Too long.*

Jaden finished stripping off his clothes, dropped them in the bin, and headed for the shower. His list of stops was growing by the minute.

****

Lara emerged from the bath, wrapped in a robe and scented of luscious sweets that tempted her appetite. It shouldn't have surprised her that a tray of canapés sat on the small table set near the window, but she took one look at it and rolled her eyes at Avelia.

"You were hungry," she explained simply. "Lunch is soon, but there is no reason for you to be hungry in the meantime."

There's no reason to be rude. "Thank you."

Avelia motioned her to the same plush chair she'd used the night before, easily within reach of the canapés, and she complied. Lara even sampled one of the mushroom and cheese canapés before the assembled ladies started talking.

Tricia opened the double pocket doors that hid an expansive closet and motioned to the choices within. "As a Reeve, your base colors will be silver and white. Ceremonial dresses will be in those colors." Her hand shifted toward the left, where shirts and pants were hung. "But there's no reason everything you wear has to comply to that. Based on what you wore in the human realm, we felt you might enjoy jeans and pants matched with white silk shirts and similar choices for daily wear."

"Instead of the more formal look Reeve typically indulges in," Jules added.

Tricia cut in again. "A Reeve who blends in with her people instead of standing out."

Jules nodded to her. "Precisely."

"I would prefer that," Lara admitted. She sampled a canapé with slices of smoked salmon on it. *Win number two.*

Tricia motioned to the closet again. "We have removed the unsuitable clothing that does not match your essence. Some of the pieces left behind were easily altered to be more to your essence than to Rachel's."

"Already?" Their patient smiles explained her oversight. "Oh...magic. I keep forgetting how that changes things. No one has to cook or clean or sew."

"Unless we wish to," Jules countered. "If there is something you like to do, there is no reason to use magic to accomplish it."

"I like to cook, but I wouldn't mind using magic to wash the dishes."

Tricia smiled. "I feel the same. Now... If you find you wish anything in particular, please say so. Mages who have visited the human realm often request choices that reflect it. T-shirts. Dresses that certain human designers create."

"I've never been a designer clothes type of person, but a few plain t-shirts would be nice." Another thought occurred to her. "And..." Her cheeks heated.

"Yes, Reeve Lara?" Jules prompted her.

"What do women in Sanctum wear for...lingerie?"

Tricia and Jules shared a knowing look. Tricia performed an intricate hand movement. "I know just the thing."

****

"Tell me," Sirena whispered across the display case top.

Jaden glanced at the shop out of the corner of his eye, noting the unusually high number of patrons who'd chosen to browse once he headed inside. The rumor mill was buzzing, and Sirena doubtless wanted the coup of having the newest, juiciest information, right from the source.

Too bad. Reeve wanted to keep Lara's existence a secret for a day or two.

He pretended to consider all the possible promise necklaces in the case, though he'd already made his decision. "Whatever do you mean?" Playing innocent wasn't something he did often, but it served its purposes.

The jeweler's eyes hardened. "Come now, Jaden. Everyone knows Rachel has been spending her days—and nights, might I add—with Borgal, and she's wearing a new promise necklace. One Borgal purchased not three days ago, in this very shop. Now you are looking for a promise necklace as well."

She hinted at the rest of the facts the entire population of Sanctum had probably discussed at length. The Mage Prophet had decreed—to the populace's mistaken understanding—that Rachel was his mate. Now Rachel had chosen Borgal, and Jaden was taking another.

"Yes, I am. May I see this one?" He indicated the one he'd chosen.

Sirena scowled at him, but she retrieved the necklace in question. It was a white gold braided chain with deep blue sapphire gems that matched Lara's eyes and a small teardrop of the same at the center. It was perfect, and it was nothing like the promise necklace he'd chosen for Rachel so long ago.

I was a child at the time. In fact, the only reason Rachel had accepted it at all was because she'd been a toddler, and the necklace had been 'pretty.' He had no doubts it irked her in her adulthood that she'd bound herself so innocently to a promise to consider him as her mate, a promise only he or her father could release her from.

She is released to her true mate now, and we are both the better for it.

"I'll take it."

She took her time, packaging it carefully, but her expression announced she was searching for inroads to continue questioning him. At last, she spoke. "The first necklace you purchased was lovely. This one is as well," Sirena hastened to add. "But I fear this one will be a poor match for Rachel."

"Since Rachel already has a promise necklace from Borgal, I cannot fathom why she would require another," he quipped.

"If I may be so bold, Jaden?"

"Please do." If she didn't ask the direct questions, someone else surely would. He wouldn't be able to last two or three days without offering what sounded like a direct answer to someone.

"Why did you release Rachel from the promise?"

"She'd never accepted the mating. There were no unbreakable vows between us. And... Any given mage should be with who makes him or her happy."

"You wouldn't have been happy with Rachel?" Her confusion required no explanation. Mates were, by definition, happy with each other. How could beings gods-crafted for each other not be?

"I can safely, and with no ill will to Rachel, state that I would not have been, and she would not have been happy with me."

"Then you believe the Mage Prophet was incorrect in naming you as mates?" There was a hint of scandal in that. "Or perhaps that Abbigell had motive to lie?"

That was harder to answer and still sound sincere. Jaden thought back to his discussion with Borgal, and the answer was obvious. "The Mage Prophet always has a plan and is rarely straightforward about it. I am sure her plan will be apparent in due time." *In two or three days.*

He passed the payment across the counter and accepted the promise necklace from Sirena. He turned to go, noting that the other patrons were already discussing what he'd said in whispers.

"Jaden?" Sirena called out to him.

He looked back in surprise. "Yes?"

"Who is the promise necklace you've chosen for? One never chooses a promise necklace until he knows the lady to fit it to her."

He smiled. "Someone I know I will be happy with."

Her jaw dropped, and Jaden made his way out of the shop. He turned toward the center of town, chuckling darkly. Every move he made would be watched now.

Everyone would be trying to guess who his secret mate was.

****

Lara smiled at the knock on the bedroom door. "Come in, Jaden."

There was a moment of hesitation. "It is Darren."

Though she was disappointed, Lara maintained her smile. "Come in," she invited again.

The door eased open, and her father entered the room. He stopped short, ranged his gaze over the white silk blouse and faded blue jeans she'd donned after her bath, and smiled. "So like your mother."

"Except her eyes and hair color," she added. "I definitely got those from you."

He closed the door and lingered near it. "I never sent people to push her away," he stated.

"Jaden explained that."

He shot her a look of longing.

"I believe you."

There was a tense moment of silence. "Did she ever...find another man?"

Lara considered that. "She went out on a few dates over the years. There was nothing serious. And before you ask... No, she never had another child."

"I wasn't going to ask it, but I probably should have." His expression was pained. "Was she happy? Were you?"

"Until Gart? Yes. We were both happy. We didn't live like this, of course." Lara motioned to the ridiculous lace and ruffles, the canopied bed, and the etchings on the walls. "We were...comfortable, but not rich. Mother said

121

she had more than she'd had before, and she didn't have to work, but we lived modestly."

"Good." It seemed there was more he wanted to say.

"Father?" It felt odd saying the word. *I've never had the opportunity to do it before.*

He winced. "My other daughters call me Daddy."

It was an offhand comment. Lara wasn't even sure he meant to speak it aloud.

"Would you rather have me call you that?"

"What?" He looked up at her, seemingly confused, then waved off the suggestion. "No. Of course not. Whatever you're comfortable with."

Lara nodded, trying to decipher what Darren was really thinking.

"I know you're going to want to live with Jaden. And that's right," he hastened to add. "I just hope you'll want to..."

"Spend time with you? Get to know you?"

He nodded solemnly.

"Of course. I think Reeve is going to keep me rather busy for the next few days, and since he wants me to stay out of sight..." She sighed. "I suppose I won't be staying with Jaden until after—"

"Of course you can."

The pronouncement stunned her to silence. It took a moment for his meaning to settle in. "You're a Transporter."

His smile was wide and heartfelt, lighting his eyes. This was the smile her mother had told her about.

"I don't think Jaden would complain about me transporting you in and out for a few days."

Lara looked at the closet, then the dresser, both of which were stuffed with clothes, thanks to Tricia and Jules. "I don't think anyone else anticipated that. All the clothes and cosmetics they've made for me have been stored here."

"Easily remedied. I'll contact the master artisan in woodworking and have him send furniture matching what Jaden already has to his home. I can move clothing as easily as I can move people."

Happiness overwhelmed her, and Lara bounced to her feet and hugged him. Darren hesitated a moment, then wrapped his arms around her.

****

Jaden sat behind Frederick's work table with him, thankful that the master artisan met with patrons in the alcove off his workshop instead of his atypically-crowded showroom.

Jaden had ordered the new drapes, sheets, quilts, and rugs for his bedroom and the new adjoining dressing room—formerly a storage room—an hour earlier. Since Jules had already been taken into their confidence, he placed the order through her and had her pass the order along to her brother. Everything would be delivered shortly after lunch, and Frederick's staff would decorate when they delivered the new furnishings.

When Jules had seen him entering her shop, a string of ladies who found they needed this or that on his heels, she'd taken him into her workroom, on the pretense that she needed to fit a new outfit for him.

Well, he'd thought it was a pretense. In fact, she'd designed his ceremonial garb. As mate to the Reeve, there were expectations as to what he would wear. Of course, the claim to need to fit it was laughable. With her expertise, the clothing fit perfectly, though Jules had only had the morning to create such a thing for him.

"What is it you need, young Dream-Walker?" Frederick asked, readying the canvas planning board he would record the order on.

"What do you have in stock...bedroom and dressing room?"

"What wood?"

"Cherry." Though there hadn't been any cabinets or dressers in the dream bedroom they'd shared, the accent pieces on the bed were cherry wood.

"Dark or light."

"Dark."

"How many pieces?"

"Four poster bed. Or sleigh, if you don't have four poster in a matched set. Vanity and chair. Two end tables. Full-length mirror. Chest. A library wall. Dressers and Cabinets."

"How many dressers and cabinets?"

"Two dressers." Women have a lot of hanging clothing. Lara is a Reeve at that, which means she'll have more than the usual. "Three cabinets."

The artisan raised a bushy brow but didn't comment. His finger motions over the canvas stopped, and he turned it toward Jaden. "I have two possible choices in stock today. This is the first. As you can see, it is a very masculine choice."

Jaden bit back a wince. It was too masculine. The furniture was heavy and inelegant. "I don't think so."

Frederick waved a hand over the canvas and another appeared. The furniture was feminine, soft curves instead of heavy blocks of wood.

"Done. This one. Can it be delivered this afternoon?" He wasn't certain what his rush was. Reeve was sure to want to keep Lara close until she'd been presented.

I don't know what time constraints I will have over the next few days. It's better to get it done now than to find out I don't have time to do it later.

A flashing green triangle in the corner of the canvas caught Jaden's eye. Frederick turned it toward him and touched it, shielding the information it revealed from Jaden.

"Do you mind, Jaden?"

"Of course not." The man had a business to run.

Frederick made a quick hand motion, read the message, and scowled. He looked up at Jaden, seemingly calculating something.

"Frederick?" Jaden prompted him.

"Why would Darren Reeveson be asking me to send an additional cabinet and dresser to match your bedroom to your home as a gift?"

He pressed his hand to the promise necklace in his pocket, clearing his throat. "Please tell Darren I would welcome the gift of him paying for those pieces in the new set I am ordering. Oh...will they be delivered this afternoon?"

Frederick stared at him for another moment. "Certainly. Since they are in stock, it should not be difficult." He sent a reply to Darren and closed the discussion box.

Then he returned the canvas to Jaden. "Place your hand in the center of the canvas. It is bespelled to help you fit the pieces to the rooms, so the delivery men can arrange the rooms as you wish."

Jaden closed his eyes and did as he was bid. The image in his mind was crisp and clear, and the spell had started him with a nearly perfect arrangement. He only had to switch the placements of two pieces of furniture before he was satisfied. As an afterthought, he added the decoration details.

Jaden opened his eyes and handed the canvas back to Frederick.

"There will be an extra charge for the decorating," the master artisan added.

"Of course."

"Done." Frederick offered his hand in agreement.

Jaden took it, satisfied with his efforts. Now it was time to return to his mate.

He exited the shop, and most of the ladies within wrapped up their business or begged off. In moments, his complement of followers were in tow.

They stopped at the gate to Reeve's property, and Jaden swallowed a laugh. They would have to guess. None of them would dare enter without a solid reason to see the Reeve.

Chapter Fourteen

"You're redecorating, I hear," Darren noted, as Jaden entered the foyer. A chuckle followed.

"And how did you expect to explain sending me such a gift?"

Lara's father glanced out the front window toward the gate. "It seems you've already caused a stir. This will only add fuel to the fires of rumor."

"Purchasing a new promise necklace will do that alone." *Especially when the entire Sanctum knows the mate they'd anticipated for me has chosen another to spend her life with.*

"They won't be leaving soon."

"Since they have followed me all over town this morning, I would have to agree." Jaden considered that. "What about the windows. If Lara looks out—"

Darren waved him off. "My father has set a spell to allow us to look out but no one to look in. Even if Lara wants to look out the windows, no one outside can see her."

"Good move."

"Good thing I've promised Lara to transport her to and from your home for the next few nights. We'll have to remind my father to put the same spell on your home."

Jaden's cock stirred at the thought of consummating in the bedroom he'd had prepared for her instead of in Rachel's bed. "Many thanks."

"I suppose I shouldn't start delivering Lara's clothing and other belongings immediately?"

He shook his head. "Frederick promised an early-afternoon delivery. Anytime after that will be ideal."

The rest was left unsaid. Delivering after Frederick's men were gone was essential if they wanted to hide the ladies' belongings being moved into his home. The colors alone would tell someone far more than they wanted to reveal about Jaden's mystery mate.

Darren pushed away from the window and looked past Jaden. Something told Jaden to turn that direction.

Lara was descending the stairs, her hair in loose curls around her face. She was dressed in a pair of faded jeans, low strappy heels, and a silk collared blouse of stunning white. He found himself speechless. She was stunning.

She sauntered to him and pressed her lips to his. Then she whispered in Jaden's ear.

His cock came alive at the news she shared.

"I've asked for the afternoon to myself. Well...*our*selves."

****

Lunch was a much less busy affair. The only people there were Reeve, Darren, herself, and Jaden.

Lara managed to focus on the food she wanted, but she forgot to focus on the drinks and had to have Jaden show her how to add that after the initial spell was cast. In the end, Reeve decided it would be easier to cast the spell itself with later additions allowed.

After the meal, she and Jaden left the table together. To Lara's relief, no one called them back or reminded them of things that needed to be accomplished.

They climbed the stairs, her heart light in anticipation. In Rachel's room, Lara turned to him and pressed to his body. The silk against her skin tantalized her senses.

Jaden didn't hesitate. One hand cupped the back of her head, and his mouth descended on hers in a hot, hard kiss.

She reached up and started undoing the buttons on her shirt, but Jaden's hands covered hers to stop her. Her disappointment was potent at that move. Were they ever going to consummate their mating?

Jaden started speaking before she could question him. "Tonight."

"But I asked for the afternoon—"

"There are three very good reasons why we can't finish right now."

That irritated her. "And those are?" she challenged.

"First... Your father is going to be moving your belongings to my home."

"Not for an hour or more." Surely, there was plenty of time to consummate before then.

He nuzzled her lips. "I don't intend on getting out of bed with you that quickly once we get in."

Her heart tripped in excitement. "I can't argue that."

"I hope not." There was a teasing note in his voice.

"What are the other two reasons?"

He glanced around, scowling at the room around them. "I would rather our first time in the physical realm be in our bedroom. This is..."

"Nauseating?" she suggested. The more Lara found herself surrounded by the frills Rachel seemed to adore, the less she liked them.

"Quite. Even if you don't like the style of my home and want to make changes, I have to believe you will be more comfortable there than here. I know I will be."

"And the last reason?" she asked. He'd said there were three.

Jaden was abruptly serious. "There is a tradition that typically precedes the consummation. For that matter, it typically precedes the promise."

Lara took a calming breath. "And we broke with this tradition," she guessed.

"We had no choice. You were dying at the time. I was hardly going to stall to see to tradition then."

"But now... I think I understand. It's not something we should skip, if we have a choice. What is this tradition?"

Jaden reached into his pocket and pulled out folded piece of dark blue velvet. With it settled on his left hand, he started unfolding it.

Lara gasped at the sight of the necklace inside. "It's beautiful."

"It's yours, if you choose to wear it."

"Why would I choose not to?"

"It's bespelled. If you agree to let me put it on, it will remain with you as a sign to others that you have a mate that you are considering...or have bound yourself to fully, when that is the case. Only Reeve or I can remove it, unless there's a life and death reason for it to be removed."

She considered that. "So...it's like a wedding band, but it can't be removed?"

He nodded solemnly.

A niggling of unease settled in.

Jaden straightened in response. "What is it?"

"Did Rachel—?"

"A different necklace. I chose it when I was eight. She accepted it when she was three. We were far too young to be giving and accepting something so monumental, but we were children who had foreknowledge—erroneous as it was—thrust upon us, so no one stopped us from doing it."

"And Reeve removed it when you found me?"

"No. I did. When I have time, I'm going to have her essence removed from the necklace by a Transient Mage. Ironically, Rachel herself would be the best person to do that, since she could benefit from her own essence. Then I will return it to the jeweler. It may be suitable for another couple."

"But not suitable for me."

He paused, a faint smile pulling up at his lips. "Look at this room, Lara."

She did that, controlling the need to wince, but only just.

"Do you think anything suited to Rachel would be suited to you? Her promise necklace was juvenile in comparison to this one, just as her room is juvenile in comparison to your tastes."

Lara nodded. "What is the tradition?"

His smile spread and lit his eyes. "I've offered this necklace as a sign of our union. If you accept it, you are announcing to all of Sanctum and beyond that you are mine. Will you allow me to place it around your neck?"

"Yes."

****

Jaden's heart stuttered at her acceptance. He'd expected more questions, more concerns about the fact that she wouldn't be able to remove the necklace.

Until she herself is Reeve.

He forced himself to calm. Since he didn't intend to give Lara any reason to want to remove the necklace, the fact that she one day would be able to shouldn't concern him.

She waited patiently for his response. Jaden lifted the necklace from the velvet wrap carefully and showed it to her. Lara brushed her fingertips over the teardrop gem, seemingly stunned.

Taking that as approval, he opened the clasp and placed the necklace at her throat. Her hand came up, and she lifted her hair away from the back of her neck to facilitate the rest. In the next heartbeat, he had it clasped.

The sense of rightness struck him. He hadn't felt anything when he'd done this with Rachel. At the time and for many years afterward, he'd attributed that to their youth. They'd been too young to take such a life-altering event seriously.

That wasn't the case now. His entire body hummed in awareness. He felt the connection between them as if it were a living, pulsing umbilical. His cock went erect, pressed tight against his jeans, and his mouth watered to taste hers.

Before he could search for a reason for the reaction, Lara was crushed against him, her mouth seeking out his. Their lips parted, tongues explored, and he ached to claim her on the nearest possible surface.

It wasn't until they ran aground on the bed that he realized they were in motion, Jaden half-guiding, half-dragging Lara along with him. His thinking mind ended there. His reasons for waiting for this evening escaped him.

As if she agreed, Lara pushed him toward the mattress, coming down over him as a pleasant, living blanket. Their mouths meshed again, a hot, hard dance that dragged a groan from him.

She played at the buttons on his shirt, and Jaden didn't protest when she unfastened them. In fact, removing their shirts sounded like a good idea, so he rolled them to their sides on the mattress and did the same for her.

The camisole beneath molded to her body like a second skin, and Jaden started working his hands beneath it.

A rush of air and the tang of magic disturbed the stillness.

"Frederick's men have— Oh shyte. My apologies."

With that pronouncement, Darren translocated away again.

Lara jerked her head up, crimson from chest to hairline. Her mouth worked as if to protest, but nothing emerged.

Jaden placed a quick kiss on her lips and pushed to his feet. Something told him Darren hadn't gone far, so it wasn't a surprise to find him outside the door, red-faced and moving in uncertain little steps.

Lara's father glanced at Jaden's bare chest and away again, clearing his throat. "My apologies," he repeated. "I forget sometimes that I shouldn't..." He circled his hand, quaking lightly.

"Have you learned your lesson?" Jaden pressed.

Darren nodded. "I think so. Should I come back later?"

Lara appeared at Jaden's side. "No. You should move everything now. Jaden and I want to make it an early night."

He swallowed down a wave of disappointment, his cock aching to finish what they'd started.

"Just don't take the bag I've set on the chair, please."

Darren and Jaden stared at her. Her father found his voice first. "Of course. But... If it's not too impertinent a question—?"

"Just a few things for tonight."

The heat in her expression made Jaden's body complain about the wait. He bit back the suggestion that they take a nap. At least that way, they would have a chance to finish what they started without the chance of Darren interrupting.

But it still wouldn't be consummation, and we both want that.

Chapter Fifteen

Lara emerged from the bathroom, dressed for the night and covered in a thick robe, the bag of her toiletries and clothes in hand.

Jaden had left for his home an hour earlier, so there'd been no temptation for him to peek at what she was wearing. Though he'd explained that he had to make a show of walking back and forth to his own house, Lara missed him when he was gone.

A light knock at the door announced that her father had arrived. "Lara? Are you ready?" he called out.

She crossed to the door and opened it, offering him a smile. "I am."

Darren nodded, took her hand, and transported them both to a strange living room. A heartbeat later, he pressed a kiss to her cheek and popped away.

Lara stood there, her mouth opened to thank him, her head spinning at his abrupt departure.

A sound behind her brought Lara's head around. Jaden was halfway down the stairs, dressed in lounging pants and a t-shirt, as he had been in her dream. Her heart stuttered in excitement, and his smile widened.

Jaden didn't hesitate. As soon as he was close enough to her, his arms closed around Lara, and his lips covered hers.

She opened for him, her heart pounding. Whatever magic—and she didn't question that it was magic—had struck them earlier was in full swing again. Unless something changed very quickly, Lara suspected the black and silver brocade sofa was about to see major action.

Jaden pulled away, gasping for breath, shaking his head as if to clear away the mindless need to christen the closest surface. "Not here." He placed a hand under her elbow and guided her to the stairs and up.

Lara padded barefoot along on the thick carpets, barely taking in her surroundings.

"We will redecorate, of course." That sounded like an apology.

"Not tonight." How could he even think about such a mundane thing when all she could think about was consummating their mating?

He chuckled darkly, stopped at a closed door, and turned to her with a raised brow. "I did take the liberty of redecorating *one* room. I hope you enjoy it."

Before she could find the words to question him, Jaden pushed the door open and waved her into it with a flourish a stage magician might use to hide his redirection.

It took a moment for the full effect to hit her. Lara ambled through the doorway and turned to take in the full effect of the room, from the four-poster bed with the chest at the foot to the end tables, bookshelves, and the vanity. The bag slipped from her boneless fingertips and landed at her feet.

She focused on the vanity again. *Already covered in my cosmetics and brushes.* "You recreated my dream room." There was no question he had.

"Not perfectly. There was no time to have the furniture recreated as you dreamed it, but it is close. And I added functional pieces of furniture that have no place in a dream bedroom." He motioned to a set of

French doors, draped in purple and blue, which were open to reveal an adjoining room.

Lara peeked inside, gaping at the fully-appointed dressing room he'd created in the same style. Words failed her again.

Jaden shifted from foot to foot. "Do you like it? We can change it if you don't."

"I love it."

He wrapped his arms around her waist, drawing Lara to the evidence that his arousal hadn't diminished in the slightest. Neither had hers.

"I see why you wanted to consummate here," she teased.

"It seemed fitting," he agreed.

"I have a surprise, too." Lara walked her fingertips up his chest.

"Do you?" His cock jerked against her through the layers separating them, leaving no doubt that he was intrigued.

She reached between their bodies and untied the belt on the robe. Jaden eased away and parted the fabric, his eyes going hot in appreciation.

Breathing was abruptly difficult.

****

Jaden didn't ask where she'd gotten such a delicious confection. Obviously, the clothiers Reeve had engaged for her had created it.

But Lara asked for this...or something *like* this. Clothiers don't produce something so personal without a request. Jaden licked his lips, savoring the view.

The baby doll nightie was sheer and silver, with a split up the front that revealed matching panties...and the fact that Adara had trimmed Lara's pubic curls. The nightie shimmered as if it was made of actual woven silver, but it moved like fabric. He suspected the shimmer was magic of some sort, perhaps a subtle glimmer.

"Do you like it?" Lara's voice was tense, and she wiggled a bit at his prolonged consideration.

"Please tell me you have more like this." He hadn't looked at the clothing Darren had delivered for her.

Her smile lit her eyes. "A few. I'm sure Adara would make me anything I like."

That was true enough, and as a young Reeve, anything Lara requested would be a priority for the artisans and businesspersons of Sanctum.

"Do you want to see more like this one?"

The need to agree beat at him, but something told him the clothiers had provided more delights to be experienced. "I think we should try them all before we decide what to order more of."

"That might take a while. I think Jules and Tricia went more than a little overboard with making me clothes. My father said one entire wardrobe is full of nothing but dresses."

Jaden laughed. "I think you'll find everyone will go that extra step for you."

"Will you?"

The invitation in her voice reminded him that they had plans. Jaden parted Lara's lips in a searing kiss. He guided her to the bed, then released her lips to lift her to the mattress.

For a moment, they stared at each other, the arousal potent. "Three steps," he vowed. Then he followed her down onto the bed.

One kiss became two...three...deeper and harder with every meeting of their lips. All the plans Jaden had painstakingly formulated for a long, slow seduction were abandoned in the heat of the moment.

Lara pulled at his t-shirt, and Jaden dragged it off and tossed it over his shoulder. She went to work at his lounging pants, and Jaden shifted away to remove her panties.

Her hand closed around his cock, stroked, then tightened and guided him toward her. Jaden thrust into her, his lounging pants still ringing his thighs and her panties at her knees.

His heart thundered, drowning out everything but Lara's cries and his own. It was over in minutes, leaving them both panting and coated in sweat. His shoulder and chest burned, most likely scratches Lara had left in the heat of the moment.

Jaden stared at her, stunned. He'd never felt anything like that before, though he'd taken a few lovers over the years. *Usually when I became frustrated enough with Rachel to seek out another woman.* That alone should have told him Rachel wasn't right for him.

Lara bit at her lower lip, rolling her hips against his with a moan. He smiled, satisfied that she was as affected by what they'd done as he was, rushed though it had undeniably been.

He whispered her name, anxious to hear what she had to say but not anxious enough to startle her out of her enjoyment.

Lara wrapped herself around him with a sigh. "More than three steps," she murmured.

"That's just the beginning." If his cock had anything to say about it, they might not get any sleep at all tonight.

****

Lara gasped as Jaden's cock erupted inside her again. She settled in his lap in the bath, face to face with him, her knees next to his hips.

The third time had been no less exciting than the two before, though they'd managed to slow down and do the many things they'd wanted to do after the mad rush of their consummation. Still, her body protested that it wasn't enough.

"Is consummation always like this?" she asked. "There has to be magic to this. People just don't...do this every day."

Jaden chuckled darkly, his cock bucking inside her. "Every consummation is different, as I understand it. Maybe ours is more potent because we didn't consummate immediately following the promise, as most people do. Maybe it's the release of the stress of your time running from Gart. I can't say why it is. I'm just glad it is."

Lara glanced toward the window beside the tub, staring at the people walking by on the street below. She'd shied at the idea of having sex next to the glass, until Jaden explained that no one outside the house could see in.

"They cannot see a thing," he reminded her patiently.

She managed a weak grin. "I know."

"Then what is wrong?"

"Nothing. I... It's just new. Magic in my life is new." She motioned to the window and turned her head to look at him. "This... This is nearly normal. Two-way glass...sort of."

Jaden smiled a wicked, little grin. His stroked up and down at her lower back. "You know, no one is going to be able to stop talking about this."

"This?"

"Who my mate is. Until Reeve makes the announcement, all of Sanctum will be speculating."

"But how would they know?"

He trailed a finger along the promise necklace. "I bought this. And... Well, I'm sure no one close enough when we've been making love will question it."

Lara shot a suspicious look at the window. "But you said they couldn't see."

He leaned close to whisper the answer in her ear. "The spell prevents them from seeing. It doesn't prevent them from hearing."

Her body reacted fiercely to that, her arousal coming to a razor edge. Jaden's eyes went hot in promise. In the next heartbeat, they were moving against each other, venting more sounds to fuel the rumors.

Chapter Sixteen

"You have many questions," Reeve stated. He sat, his hands steepled in front of his face, waiting for her reply.

Lara considered what to ask first. There were so many possibilities, it was difficult to order them all. Finally, she chose one. "I'm supposed to lead. How am I supposed to do that? What am I responsible for?"

A sly smile curved his lips up. "That is not what you really want to know."

It was. She furrowed her brow, questioning him silently.

"I had Juniatta do some...investigation for me at breakfast yesterday. I hope you can forgive that, but it was essential for me to know what would set your mind at ease."

"But I do want to know the answers to those questions."

"You do, but first, there are more important questions for me to answer. Those can come later." He waited for something nameless.

It took a minute for his meaning to become clear. "What precisely happened to Gart?" Just saying his name made her nervous.

Reeve nodded and settled slightly forward in his chair, resting his hands on his thighs. "I should tell you first that it was relatively painless. Certainly less pain than he inflicted on you or even on Jaden."

She nodded.

"Borgal kept Gart busy...fighting, while Darren took Rachel to the rogue's back. Rachel's power is somewhat similar to that of a Reeve, but her magic specifically affects magical essence. She can take magical essence from a mage, and she can give magical essence to another mage to use."

"She can drain someone's power and charge someone else to make that person more powerful?" *That could be very useful.*

"Temporarily. Even a very powerful Transient Mage cannot permanently remove or grant magical essence. Since the body makes the essence constantly, the...drained mage will replenish in time, and the mage gifted will expend the magic and only be able to replace at his or her own rate."

"I think I understand that. So... Rachel drained Gart." She didn't question it.

"As much as she could stand to. Since Rachel is a young mage, her ability to siphon off essence is limited to touch and the amount she can store without directly passing it to another is similarly limited."

"And then?"

"She passed some of Gart's magical essence to Darren as she siphoned it off to replenish him. When she'd reached her limit...and he reached his, Darren transported her to the other side of the room, leaving Gart diminished. She laid hands on myself and Borgal to give us as much of Gart's essence to fuel our efforts as possible.

"The combination made Borgal more powerful than Gart was. Not that Borgal was losing in his bid to dispatch Gart personally." Reeve smiled a wry little smile.

"And then?"

"I used the Reeve's power to rip Gart's soul from his physical body and push it all the way to the afterlife."

Lara shuddered at the concept.

"Nearly painless," Reeve reminded her. "Left alive, Gart would have replenished himself and gone on to kill others."

She nodded. "I suppose that's true."

"A Reeve does not kill unless there is the most pressing of reasons to do so. Only to protect life of those within Sanctum...and outside, at his own discretion."

"But he or she can banish someone for much less." It was out before she could stop herself from saying something so impertinent. Her face heated.

Reeve sighed. "Juniatta warned me that you had concerns about that." He paused, seemingly collecting his thoughts. "What the rogue told you was only partially true."

"Which part?"

"There was a plague. Both my father and Gart lost their mates. My father did request Eviana as his wife. She had a choice, and she chose to become my father's wife and give him heirs."

"Did she love Gart?"

"Remember that I knew her years later. She loved my father...then. I cannot say with certainty if she loved Gart and chose my father out of duty to provide heirs to the Reeve and came to love him with time or if she preferred him to Gart then. I can tell you that no one forced Eviana to become my father's wife."

Lara considered that. "Why would she see it as a duty?"

"Gart already had an heir."

"Borgal." Jaden had explained their connection to her.

"Yes. Gart had an heir, but my father didn't have one. His mate died while she was carrying his first child. The power of the Reeve passes through the family line."

"If he didn't have children, there wouldn't be a Reeve." It was starting to make more and more sense.

"Precisely. My mother produced two children for my father. There had to be an heir to the Reeve's power."

"Then I have a great-aunt or great-uncle somewhere?" *Cousins? How large was the family?*

Reeve shook his head. "My brother was killed in an accident in the human realm years ago. Knowing about Gart's attempts... I suspect the rogue may have been involved. He would have wanted to prevent any unexpected heirs to the Reeve wherever he could. He probably planned to kill Darren as well...until he found out about you."

"I was a more direct route to what he wanted to accomplish."

He nodded, seemingly weary. "Ingenious but horrific."

Silence fell between them.

Reeve settled back in his chair again. "Have I answered your questions about the rogue to your satisfaction?"

Lara nodded. "I believe so."

"Good. Then we will return to the original questions you posed. A Reeve is responsible for safety and for justice."

"And how does he or she do that?"

His smile said it was going to be an extended lesson.

Chapter Seventeen

Lara fidgeted, straightening the long, silver gown for the third time in as many minutes. She fussed with the black sash belt, though Tricia's magic held it in place and would for the length of the day, she was sure. Jaden chuckled and shook his head.

She wanted to say something snarky in return, but the sight of him in the black suit with the silver silk Mandarin shirt stilled her tongue. He was gorgeous, too much so for her piece of mind today.

It was early, and the day had already been a long one. Darren had popped into their home during breakfast, joined them for a slice of toast, and transported her to Reeve's home. There, she'd been primped and powdered and dressed in finery, while Jaden made an unobtrusive walk to Reeve's home, dressed in his usual ceremony clothing, probably to keep the citizenry guessing at the announcement of the day.

And the day has barely begun.

A sharp knock on the door made her jump, and Jaden sighed and crossed the room to hug her. He didn't repeat that she had nothing to worry about. He'd said it countless times in the last day.

"Come in," she called at last.

The door opened, and Reeve came in, followed by Darren. The two stopped and smiled.

Lara separated from Jaden slowly. "It's time, I guess."

Reeve tipped his head. "Just as we discussed. I will leave first, starting the procession into town."

She nodded. "Rachel and Borgal will meet you halfway and join in. Darren will transport us to the stage, then go to his house to join the procession further down."

Reeve dropped a kiss on one cheek. Darren did the same on the other cheek. Then her grandfather strolled out of the room and down the stairs.

Lara went to the window and watched Reeve walk down the path and through the front gate of his estate, straightening the sleeves of his all-white tux. People waiting outside the gate dropped in behind him, jockeying for position close to their leader.

"Ready to go?" Darren asked.

Lara nodded and returned to Jaden's side. He took her hand, and Darren laid one of his over both of theirs. In the next moment, they were standing behind the drape on the presentation stage erected for the event. Darren pulled his hand back and motioned for silence. Then he clicked his heels smartly and transported away.

Lara felt the urge to laugh at that. She stifled it, reminding herself that crowds were already forming outside.

Jaden put a finger to his lips as if in reminder, his eyes sparkling in mischief. He leaned close to her and parted Lara's lips in a slow, sweet kiss. The kiss grew deeper and hotter by the moment.

Cheers from outside startled Lara, and she started smoothing her clothing. Reeve was coming, and she would be a mess for her presentation to the people she had to learn to lead.

Jaden leaned to whisper in her ear. "With the non-wrinkle spells on your clothes and the non-smudge spells on your cosmetics, there is nothing to fix. You look perfect."

Lara felt her cheeks darken. She took a calming breath and nodded her agreement. He was correct. Jules and Tricia had explained all of that to her. It was an attack of nerves and nothing more.

Reeve started talking from the front of the stage, his voice projected by means she suspected had nothing to do with amps and speakers and microphones.

"Welcome. Welcome. Welcome. I am certain you are all wondering why I have called you here today."

The crowd let out another cheer in response.

"Never let it be said I am one to disappoint."

Claps and whistles punctuated that statement.

"My dear Daza blessed me with two children. This week, my daughter Rachel has bound herself to her mate, Borgal."

There was a moment of silence, probably in confusion or shock at that pronouncement.

Reeve continued as if he hadn't noticed it. "Many years ago, the Mage Prophet Abbigell made a prophecy that my eldest female heir would be fated for Jaden. That tale has been spread far and wide, all throughout Sanctum and beyond."

He paused, and murmurs rose in the crowd.

Finally, someone dared shout out a question. "Did the Mage Prophet speak falsely, Reeve?"

Reeve didn't answer. No one asked another question, probably out of fear of asking the one that Reeve would find most offensive. It was a safe bet no one wanted to suggest Daza had taken a lover while she was mated to Reeve.

"Other news reached me this week. Surprising news. Shocking, in some ways. You see, I found I am a grandfather three times over and not two."

The crowd erupted in a cacophony of sounds.

The drape opened, revealing Lara and Jaden to the assembled residents of Sanctum. A hush fell over the crowd, and everyone turned to stare at her. A few heads swiveled back and forth, no doubt comparing her to Rachel, who stood at her father's side, dressed in a deep blue dress that nicely complemented Borgal's deep brown clothing. A few gasps turned into more. Heads slanted toward each other, and whispers ran the length and breadth of the assembled crowd.

Jaden took Lara's arm and guided her to the front of the stage, where Reeve raised her gloved hand and kissed her knuckles gently. She managed a rather shaky curtsey, as she'd been instructed to greet him.

"People of Sanctuary... May I introduce my eldest female heir, Lara Reeveson, mate to Jaden Koleson...and your young Reeve."

The wave of shouts and claps died out for a moment as his final words sank in fully. There was a full minute of stomach-clenching silence before they erupted again.

Here and there, she heard comments passing.

"I made the young Reeve's new furniture."

"And I her accent pieces."

"I saw Jaden choose her promise necklace. I did. I swear it."

"She did. At my shop. I made the promise necklace Jaden chose."

Lara smiled at their excitement.

Questions followed.

"Who is her mother, Reeve?"

"Reeve Lara, will you tell us how you came to Sanctum?"

"How did you meet Jaden, Reeve Lara?"

Her head spinning, Lara wasn't certain where to begin, and the questions kept coming.

Reeve raised his arms, and silence fell. "A banquet. Tonight, to celebrate both matings. Reeve Lara will speak to you all then."

Lara nodded and raised a hand in a wave.

Reeve nodded to someone behind her. A hand closed on Lara's shoulder and a second on Jaden's...and they appeared in their living room.

Darren laughed. "That will keep them busy all day, buying gifts...trading rumors and stories...dressing for the ceremony. See you tonight."

Before Lara could answer, her father was gone.

She sighed. "He really has to learn to use proper hellos and goodbyes."

Jaden wrapped his arms around her. "And respect boundaries," he added.

Her chuckle choked off at a light knocking at the front door. "Reeve?" she guessed.

He shook his head. "No. I'd wager it's the only other people in Sanctum who would dare disturb us before the banquet."

Jaden strode to the door without explaining his comment, and Lara smoothed her dress again, a useless endeavor that she cursed the moment she'd done it.

He turned back with a smile, waving a couple who shared Jaden's dark features into their home. The two had barely cleared the door when they bowed deeply to Lara and didn't rise.

"Please. Don't," she breathed. These were obviously family of Jaden's. It didn't feel right to her to have them bowing this way.

They straightened.

"As you wish," the man assured her with a tip of his head.

Jaden didn't hesitate. "Lara... These are my parents, Kole and Nina."

There was a moment of stillness. Then Jaden's mother rushed across the room and folded Lara in her arms.

"Welcome, Reeve Lara. Welcome to Sanctum and to our family."

"Is it really necessary for your parents to call me Reeve?" she asked Jaden.

He shook his head. "Not until you rule Sanctum. They are family, after all."

"Then don't, please," she requested.

"As you wish," Kole replied again.

Lara backed away from Nina with a sigh. "There's no helping that, I suppose."

Jaden's mother smiled warmly and placed her hand against Lara's cheek. "He'll calm down in time. This was just such a surprise for us." She shot a long-suffering look at Jaden and lowered her hand. "You could have told us, Jaden."

"You could have visited," he suggested smoothly, in a voice that said he was teasing his mother.

"I tried, and you were with Reeve. I could hardly intrude."

Jaden planted a kiss on her cheek. "My apologies."

His father looked around the room. "I see your mate has not had a chance to make her mark on your home."

Lara felt her cheeks heat. She'd certainly made her mark on the bedroom furnishings.

"Most of the house," Jaden agreed. "Now that our mating has been announced, we'll have time to see to that."

"Don't purchase too much," Kole counseled. "Everyone will want to give gifts to the young Reeve and her mate. It's guaranteed that all the artisans in Sanctum will want to make personalized gifts of furniture, jewelry that match the promise necklace, decorations, and all sorts of other baubles."

Nina nodded. "I imagine you'll be spending a considerable amount of time in consultations over the next month or two." She paused only a moment. "Which reminds me... I should get a feel for what you might like our gift to be."

Lara started to protest that it wasn't necessary for them to give a gift.

Jaden wrapped an arm around her and tilted his head toward hers. "It will offend her if you refuse. Mother loves using her power to make others happy."

She nodded. "All right then. What do we have to do?"

Nina hooked her arm through Lara's and led her to the sofa in the living room. She sat on one end and had Lara sit on the other. With Lara's hands enfolded in hers, Nina closed her eyes.

Warmth raced from her hands, up Lara's arms and chest, enveloped her neck and then her head. In the next moment, her head spun sickly.

Lara found herself in Jaden's arms, gasping for breath. Across the room, Nina was nestled to her husband's chest, shaking.

"My apologies, Lara. I didn't know."

She shook her head, trying to right her senses. What had happened? What was Nina apologizing for?

Jaden tensed. "No. It was my fault. I owe both of you an apology. I should have warned you, Mother."

"I don't understand," Lara managed.

"It probably happened too quickly for Lara to process what was happening to her," Kole inserted.

Jaden nodded. "That makes sense."

"Process what?" Lara asked.

"Mother's magic allows her to see people's pasts."

She winced at what Nina might have seen.

"I would like to offer you a gift, Lara." Nina's offer sounded stiff and formal.

Jaden settled on the sofa with Lara in his lap. "We would welcome whatever gift you offer. You know that."

"Other artisans will wish to do a similar examination on you to choose a gift."

Lara closed her eyes. "I'd rather not have a gift. No offense intended to you, of course. Or them."

"Which is why my offered gift may be of some use to you."

She levered her eyes open and stared at Nina. "What gift?"

"I wish to act as your proxy. If you would allow me, I will pass information on your likes...and Jaden's along to artisans and others who wish to purchase a gift."

"But that will take a lot of your time." It wasn't right to ask this of her.

"Are you refusing the gift?"

I'll offend her. "Of course not. I'd...appreciate it."

Nina tipped her head. "Very well. I will let the artisans know that I will be acting as proxy immediately."

"Now? But you just got here."

"People will want to start planning for gifts or even buy something today."

"Okay. Thank you for this gift." She meant it. Whatever had happened in those lost moments had left her exhausted.

Nina and Kole shot each other a smile, crossed the room to press kisses to Lara's forehead, and left with a promise to see her at the celebration.

In the aftermath, Jaden stood and started walking, Lara still in his arms.

"Where are we going?" she murmured.

"After that, you'll need to sleep for a while."

She yawned. "We'll have to call Tricia and Jules and—"

"Magic," he reminded her.

"Mmm hmm." She was sound asleep before he reached the bedroom.

****

The hall was on the outskirts of town. It was a huge building, surrounded by expansive gardens.

Lara hesitated at the doorway, gaping. "How often can they possibly need to use this?"

Jaden smiled. "It's not always here. Reeve calls it forth when the need arises."

"Like a pop-up tent."

He chuckled darkly. "Very much like that."

The closest people went silent at her entrance. The stillness moved like a wave over the crowd. They stood and tipped their heads respectfully. After a moment, they started closing on her position, reaching out to touch her as Lara and Jaden passed between the rows of people.

Reeve met them at the head of the room and ushered Lara to the seat next to his. Jaden took the next further chair, Reeve settled in his own, and Lara took a calming breath as the people of Sanctum gathered around.

There was no pushing and shoving. There were no shouted questions. The people formed snaking lines behind the two individuals centered in front of her.

They took turns, coming forward in singles, couples, and family groups. There was no need to explain the story of her past. It seemed Nina had taken it upon herself to explain that, as Lara's proxy.

Every one of the family groups or individuals offered gifts. The three jewelers of Sanctum offered earrings, bracelets, and rings that matched her promise necklace. The master artisan offered furnishings for their living room. Others offered furnishings for other rooms, clothing for children they would someday have together, and various baubles and promises of fitting gifts at the appropriate times for them in the future.

Lara thanked them, spoke with each for a few moments, and moved along to the next.

The last to come forward was Jaden's parents. Kole was holding a gift in his hands and smiling widely.

Lara's cheeks heated. "You've already given me a gift," she protested.

"No," Kole corrected her. "Nina has. I haven't offered mine yet."

She started to protest, then stopped. It will offend him if I refuse. Lara searched for the words Jaden had used earlier. "We would welcome any gift you offer."

Kole offered a tip of his head and handed over the present.

Lara took her time opening it, furrowing her brow at the thick book inside. She opened the book. It took a moment for the first page to come into focus. The truth wrenched a gasp from her lips, and Lara touched the image with shaking fingers, tears welling up in her eyes.

"What is it?" Jaden asked.

She tipped the book his direction, at a loss for words.

His gaze trailed over the page then lighted on her. "That's your mother. Isn't it?"

Lara nodded, and a tear splashed to her cheek. "I thought Gart had destroyed everything. I couldn't take the pictures when I ran, and I heard about the fire that destroyed my home." She swallowed hard.

A handkerchief appeared in Kole's hand, and he reached out to wipe the tear away. "He may have, but I am capable of recreating what was lost from Nina's memories. She shared with me what was most prominent in your memories."

Lara handed the book to Jaden and wrapped her arms around Kole. "Most gladly welcome," she assured him. "I can't thank you enough."

****

"Why does the gift trouble you?"

Lara looked up at Juniatta in surprise, her face flushing in embarrassment. "I suppose... I didn't really know my mother, did I?"

She settled into Jaden's empty chair. "Not being in a position to know your mother at all, I cannot say how much of the real woman you knew and how much was a fabrication. I suspect, being a mother personally, that you saw more of the real woman than Darren did. If something conflicts, I would assume your recollections true to the woman."

There was a tension in her that showed in her stiff posture. "Why does the gift put you on edge?" Lara countered.

Juniatta opened her mouth as if to protest, then snapped it shut. She didn't offer an answer.

"It has something to do with how you feel about my father, doesn't it?"

The Mind Healer nodded and glanced Darren's way.

"You're a mother. Is your child...?"

Juniatta sighed. "One of Darren's other daughters. Yes. She is."

"You love him," Lara guessed.

"I do, but he still clings to the idea that your mother was his mate."

"She wasn't?" It was the first time anyone had expressed doubts about it to Lara.

Juniatta shook her head. "No. Darren was young, and he looks back on that time with unrealistic filters on his memories."

"It sounds like something a Mind Healer could help him with." Lara offered a smile of encouragement.

The older woman darkened and shot a quick glance at Darren's back. "He is already a patient of mine. When he feels troubled."

Lara considered that. "Then maybe this is something I should help with."

By Juniatta's reaction, Lara guessed she considered that nothing short of scandalous. "Whatever do you mean?"

"Let me think about it."

She withdrew with a hasty dip of her head and rushed to the opposite side of the room.

Jaden returned from his discussion with Darren and offered her a glass of wine. Lara stared at her father, considering her options.

"Is something wrong, Lara?" her mate inquired, his gaze following the line of hers to Darren.

"I think my father may need a bit of a nudge." More like a shove. It had worked once before. It could work again.

"To what?"

She smiled and clicked glasses with him. "Just an experiment. A job my new duties call for," she assured him. It was the Reeve's job to abolish discord within Sanctum. This was probably the best place to start she could have hoped for.

Stand by for more stories from

Sanctum...

About the Author

Brenna Lyons wears many hats, sometimes all on the same day: former president of EPIC, author of more than 100 published works, owner of Fireborn Publishing, columnist, special needs teacher, wife, mother...and member in good standing of more than 60 writing advocacy groups.

In her first ten years published in novel-length, she's won 3 EPIC e-Book Awards (out of 15 finalists) and finaled for 3 PEARLS (including one Honorable Mention, second to NY Times Bestseller Angela Knight), 2 CAPAS, and a Dream Realm Award. She's also taken Spinetingler's Book of the Year for 2007.

Brenna writes in 26 established worlds plus stand-alones, poetry, articles and essays. She's a bestseller in indie/e fantasy and horror, straight genre and cross-genres thereof. Brenna has been termed "one of the most deviant erotic minds in the publishing world...not for the weak." (Rachelle for Fallen Angels Reviews) Milieu-heavy dark work is practically Brenna's calling card, with or without the erotic content.

She teaches classes in everything from POV studies to advanced editing, networking to marketing. Brenna enjoys hearing from people who read her work and can be reached by e-mail.

Website: http://www.brennalyons.com/

Facebook: http://www.facebook.com/brenna.lyons

Email: brennalyons4168@live.com

Maher Men
The Blutjagdfrau Chronicles
Veriel's Tales I: Crossbearer Turned
Veriel's Tales II: Losing Regana

URBAN GRIMM
Catch Me, If You Can
Three Wishes
Temptation of Eve

WEREWOLF U
Werewolf U
Younger Daughter
Alpha Son
Never Alone
Her Christmas Wolves

ANGEL-WING SAGA
Sons of Heaven: Beldon
Sons of Heaven: Unexpected Mates
Daughters of Man: Prize Match
Daughters of Man: Claiming a Princess

COLOR OF LOVE
The Color of Love

KEGIN SERIES
Conquest
The Last of Fion's Daughters
Last Chance for Love
Rites of Mating
In Her Ladyship's Service
Matchmaker's Misery

KIELAN SERIES
The Lady's Lowborn Lover
Time Currents
Cubed

STAR MAGES
Written in the Stars

The Master's Lover

DAN AIDAN FAIRIES
Fairy Dreams
Monsters of Myth Anthology

XXAN WAR
Daahan Rising
Raashh Decisions

MYTHOS SERIES
The Punishment of Phoebus Apollo
Black Sail

IT'S ALL GREEK TO ME...
All's Fair...

SANCTUM
Dream Walk

GRELLAN WAR
With Great Power

BLOOD MAGES
Enslaved

CARSON COUSINS
All I Want for Christmas is You

FATES WAR
Fates Magic

Beyond the Veil
Mine for the Night
Once in a Blue Moon
Overtime Pay
Stay With Me
The Fire God's Woman
Nevermore
Bride Ball
Undead in Blue

Mama's Tales
Unexpected Daddy
We Shall Live Again
May the Best Man Win
Marked
And It Was Good
Monsters of Myth Anthology

Available from **Under The Moon**

Evil Overlords Union Issue #1 Anthology
Undead Embrace
"Playing Games" in *Forbidden Love: Bad Boys*
"Marked" in *Forbidden Love: Wicked Women*
"The Master's Lover" in *Forbidden Love: Sacred Bands*

Available from **Logical Lust**

"Mine for the Night" in *The Cougar Book* Anthology

Available from **Coming Together Charity Anthologies**

INSTINCT SERIES
"Foundling" in *Coming Together: Into the Light* Anthology

"Claim Mate" (available separately and as part of the *Coming Together: Against the Odds* Anthology)
"The Fire God's Woman" in *Coming Together: Under Fire* Anthology

Available *self-published*

Snapshots from a Poet's Life

Award-Winning Books

EPPIE/EPIC eBOOK AWARDS WINNERS
Coming Together: Against the Odds- 2010
Time Currents- 2010
Coming Together: Into the Light- 2011

EPPIE/EPIC eBOOK AWARDS FINALISTS
Fion's Daughter- 2004
Collected Poems: Book One- 2005 (now titled *Snapshots of a Poet's Life*)
Renegade's Run- 2005
Rites of Mating- 2006
All I Want for Christmas- 2006
Phaze in Verse- 2008
"The Fire God's Woman" in Coming Together: Under Fire- 2009
Three Wishes- 2010
Matchmaker's Misery- 2010
The Cougar Book- 2011
The Master's Lover- 2011
Bride Ball- 2011

DREAM REALM AWARDS FINALIST
Last Chance for Love- 2003

PEARL HONORABLE MENTION
Night Warriors- 2004

PEARL FINALISTS
Schente Night- 2003 (now included in *The Last of Fion's Daughters*)
König Cursebreakers- 2004 (now titled *Will of the Stone*)

JOYFULLY REVIEWED BEST BOOKS OF 2010
Written in the Stars- 2010

SPINETINGLER'S BOOK OF THE YEAR 2007
NOBODY: An Anthology of Dark Fiction- 2007 (Brenna's pieces of the anthology can be found in *Beyond the Veil*)

TRS's CAPA FINALISTS
Ultimate Warriors- 2004 (Brenna's portion is now available as *With Great Power*)
Written in the Stars

LOVE ROMANCE AND MORE CAFÉ BOOK OF THE YEAR
RUNNER UP
Last Chance for Love- 2008

ROAD TO ROMANCE REVIEWERS' CHOICE AWARD
Prophecy: Revelations- 2004

LOVE ROMANCES REVIEWERS' CHOICE AWARD
Black Sail- 2003

ROMANCE JUNKIES BOOK CLUB STAFF PICK
TYGERS- 2003

FALLEN ANGELS ROMANCE RECOMMENDED READ
Devon's Price-2005 (now available in *Bearing Armen*)

JOYFULLY RECOMMENDED READ
Fairy Dreams- 2008
The Last of Fion's Daughters- 2009

TREBLE HEART FINALIST
Prophecy: Revelations- 2003

www.ingramcontent.com/pod-product-compliance
Lightning Source LLC
Chambersburg PA
CBHW021156130626
46554CB00005B/1844